THE MAGIC BOTTLE

The stairs did not end with the corridor

THE
MAGIC BOTTLE

by

CYRIL HARE

with illustrations by
W. TURNER LORD

faber and faber

This edition first published in 2008
by Faber and Faber Ltd
3 Queen Square, London WC1N 3AU

A CIP record for this book is available from the British Library

ISBN 978-0-571-24778-3

CONTENTS

CHAPTER ONE

PHILIP AND MARY

M r. and Mrs. Jelf lived with their two children in a small house just outside a village called Little Bolster, which is about twenty-five miles from London. Mr. Jelf used to take the bus every morning to

Bedstead Junction where he caught the train to the City. Sometimes he used to say when he got home in the evening that the railway was a nightmare, but as a matter of fact it was the Southern.

The children's names were Philip and Mary. Philip's birthday was in April and Mary's was in January, so for nearly three months every year Mary was only a year younger than Philip, though for the rest of the time he was two years older. When she wanted to annoy Philip between their birthdays, Mary used to go about saying that he was only a year older than she was, and quite often she would get visitors to believe it, because she was rather tall for her age and Philip was the short, thick kind.

One September, when Philip was nearly ten and a half and Mary was not quite eight and three quarters, they were both at home for the summer holidays. By rights, they ought to have been just coming back from the seaside, but this year, just when they were all getting ready to go, Philip had come out with mumps and by the time he had finished and Mary was out of quarantine it was too late, because Mr. Jelf had to go back to the City and anyway the rooms at the sea were let to somebody else. So what with one thing and another the holidays had been rather dull and Philip and Mary spent a lot of time wishing that something would happen. As a matter of fact, that was what Mr. and Mrs. Jelf were beginning to wish, but the particular thing they wanted to happen was for the holidays to stop and the children to go back to school—which is a pretty dreadful thing for anybody to wish, and only shows what awful consequences even a silly illness like mumps can have.

There was still a week of the holidays to go when something did happen. It was in the afternoon, and Philip was reading *The Arabian Nights* while Mary was looking out of the window wondering whether it was ever going to stop raining, when a car drew up outside the door and Mary said, "I believe that's Granny's car."

Granny was Mrs. Jelf's mother, and her name was Mrs. Thwaites. She was not a bit like grandmothers in films, who are always very infirm and aged, and either walk about with a stick or sit in rocking chairs knitting things and wearing large horn-rimmed spectacles. The only kind of stick Mrs. Thwaites ever used was a shooting-stick, which she took to sit on when she went to the races. She never sat in a rocking chair and she was much better at driving a car than knitting—although she could knit when she had to. In fact, she could do most things and she had a habit of doing them when you least expected, like driving over to call on the Jelfs that afternoon without ringing up to say she was coming.

Mary let her grandmother in—she got to the front door first because Philip was still in the middle of *The Arabian Nights* and it took him some time to get back— and then Mrs. Jelf came out of the kitchen. Her hands were rather floury, because she had been making a cake. (The Jelfs had a cook, whose name was Mrs. Marrable, but she had said that mumps or no mumps, she was going for her holiday, so that was that.) Then Mrs. Jelf asked her mother if she was staying to tea, but Mrs. Thwaites said No, she had only looked in for a moment and anyhow she had a picnic basket in the car. It seemed a funny sort of day to choose for a picnic, but Philip and Mary thought it wiser not to mention it, because even if Mrs. Thwaites was rather young for a grandmother, she was old enough to do what she liked without having to make excuses.

Then Mrs. Thwaites lit a cigarette (which is another thing grandmothers in films don't generally do) and said,

"I've bought Bolster Place, and I'm moving in next week."

Mrs. Jelf just said "Oh!" and did her best not to look surprised. Actually, there was very little Mrs. Thwaites could do which would surprise her, simply because nobody could tell what she was going to do next, so it was no use wondering. When they were by themselves Mr. and Mrs. Jelf used to call her "H.M.S. Unpredictable", but they fondly hoped that the children didn't know that.

Philip and Mary, who were not so good at disguising their feelings as their mother was, said "Ooh!" which is a lot more expressive than just "Oh!" They both knew Bolster Place quite well. It was a rambling old house about two miles away on the road to Featherbed, the next village to Little Bolster as you go away from London. It looked very nice from the outside, all covered with creepers, and from the road you could see that it had a kitchen garden with a wall right round it and an orchard and a big lawn with a sun-dial in the middle. But they had never been inside, because old Mrs. Worsley-Worsley, whom it belonged to, was an invalid who never had any visitors except the doctor. But at last the doctor had told her that she would never get any better unless she went to live in South Devon (which was very honourable

of him, because of course he couldn't go on attending to her after she had gone) and Mrs. Worsley-Worsley had departed in a large green ambulance and there had been a grand sale of all her furniture and finally the desirable residence—which was Bolster Place—had been put up for sale and Mrs. Thwaites had bought it.

"I am going over there now", Mrs. Thwaites said, "to measure the floors and windows to see where my carpets and curtains are going. I thought perhaps the children would like to come over and help me, unless they have anything more amusing to do this afternoon."

Mrs. Jelf looked a little doubtful and asked whether they would be home to tea, and Mrs. Thwaites said certainly they wouldn't and what did she think the picnic basket was for? There was tea in it for four hungry people if she could supply some milk. So that was all settled and Philip and Mary piled into their grandmother's car while their mother went back to finish making her cake.

In the car they found an elderly man who their grandmother introduced to them as Mr. Chaffers. Evidently he was the fourth hungry person the tea had been provided for. He did not look particularly hungry. He had very round rosy cheeks and a bald head and a small grey beard. There was a two foot rule sticking out of his coat pocket and when he was addressed he said "Ah!" in a deep, ruminating voice.

CHAPTER TWO

BOLSTER PLACE

★

It was a great moment for Philip and Mary when they drove into the grounds of Bolster Place and saw the sun-dial and the kitchen garden wall at close quarters at last. But they felt a little disappointed when their grandmother unlocked the door and they walked inside. Any house can't help looking rather dismal when it is completely empty of everything except dirt and cobwebs. The rooms looked uncomfortably large and their footsteps on the bare floors waked doleful echoes from the walls. It was difficult to imagine that it was all soon to be filled with Mrs. Thwaites's familiar furniture and that this was going to be the drawing-room and that was going to be the dining-room, when at the moment there was nothing to distinguish one from another except the varying tints of Mrs. Worsley-Worsley's faded wall-paper.

But Mrs. Thwaites seemed to have no difficulty in imagining any of these things. In no time she was down on her knees on the dusty floors, making measurements with a long tape she had brought with her, and even marking off in chalk just where sideboards and wardrobes were to stand, so that the removal men would know where to put them when they came and not find at the last moment that there was no room for something in the place intended for it, which is what is always apt to happen when you move house unless you have taken precautions beforehand. While she was doing this, Mr. Chaffers was shinning up and down a step-ladder with marvellous agility for one of his years, running his rule up and down windows, writing down figures in a very

dog-eared note-book with a pencil that lived behind his left ear, and remarking "Ah!" at frequent intervals.

Mary helped her grandmother by holding one end of the tape for her and drawing rather wobbly chalk lines across the floor. Philip steadied the step-ladder for Mr. Chaffers and retrieved his pencil when it escaped from behind his ear, which it frequently did when he leaned over at an angle to get his rule across a particularly large window. They were all pretty hot and grimy by the time Mrs. Thwaites clapped her hands and called "Time!" for tea.

There was nothing to sit on in the house, so they brought in the seats out of the car and put them on the floor in a circle round the picnic basket and sat on them cross-legged. Philip remarked that it was like a feast in *The Arabian Nights*.

"Much nicer," said Mary. "I'm sure the Arabians didn't have marmite sandwiches, or hot tea out of thermos bottles."

"Silly," said Philip, "I didn't mean that. I meant the way we are all squatting on the floor, instead of sitting up in chairs. Not that it isn't a magnificent feast, too," he added politely to his grandmother.

"If this was the Arabian Nights," said Mrs. Thwaites, "perhaps my Turkey carpet would be a flying one. Then I could get it to float over here and see if it really will fit in to the hall. I'm sure I've got the measurements wrong."

"Ah!" said Mr. Chaffers with his mouth full of cake. He didn't explain what he meant, and presently he got up, brushed the crumbs off his waistcoat and wandered back to his step-ladder. Mrs. Thwaites collected up the tea-things and then said that as the Turkey carpet was evidently not in a mood for flying, she was going to measure the hall again, just in case. Philip and Mary took the seats to the car and returned to the house. They were both getting rather tired of chalking and measuring, though they didn't like to say so. But Mrs. Thwaites had a knack of guessing what people were thinking without their speaking or even apparently without looking at them, for while she was still on her knees on the floor trying to read the figures on the tape, she remarked, "I expect you children would like to do some exploring, wouldn't you? There's quite a lot of the house you haven't seen yet. I'll call you when we're ready to go."

Off went the children, raising clouds of dust as they raced each other up the stairs. Mrs. Thwaites was perfectly right, they soon found. There certainly was a lot of the house they hadn't seen, or wouldn't even have suspected, looking at it from the front. The front rooms, which they had been in already, were just ordinary straightforward rooms, with four walls at right angles to one another and a door and windows where you would expect to find them. But at the back of the house things became much more interesting. The rooms there seemed to have been tucked in wherever the builder could find room for them, so that they were of all shapes and sizes, but mostly quite small. Some had ceilings that sloped unexpectedly, or beams that caught the unwary head. There was a corridor that ran the length of the house, with dark corners which were apt to conceal steps up or down with fatal results to the rash explorer. And everywhere were odd bits of things left behind from the furniture sale—broken bedroom chairs and towel-horses with missing legs, scraps of carpet and linoleum—enough, they thought, for a good sized bonfire the next fine day they found themselves at Bolster Place.

At the very end of the corridor was a flight of stairs. Going down it, they found themselves back in the kitchen which they had already seen. They lingered long enough at the bottom to hear Mr. Chaffers still booming "Ah!" from the window of what was to be the dining-room. They returned to the top, and saw that the stairs did not end with the corridor, but continued upwards for another two or three steps and came to a full stop in front of a low door. It took quite a tug to open it and then they found themselves looking into a long, low room with a steep-pitched raftered roof. The air smelled musty, as though the small window at the far end, which let in what little light there was, had not been opened for some time.

"What d'you think this is?" said Mary.

"Box-room," said Philip. "I remember the advertisement of the house said: 'Five principal bed and dressing-rooms, day and night nurseries, three maids' rooms, roomy attics and box-room.' This must be it."

"I can see a box in the far corner there now," said Mary, peering about in the gloom. "I wonder why Mrs. Worsley-Worsley left it behind."

"Because it wasn't worth taking, I expect," Philip suggested. "Like the towel-horses and junk in the roomy attics, or whatever they were. We might have a look at it, all the same."

He took a step across the floor and immediately there was a "chink" of falling glass.

"Look out!" said Mary, whose eyes were better than Philip's, though naturally he would never admit it. "I can see now. The floor is simply covered with bottles."

Mary was exaggerating, of course. It was a large room, and, as they afterwards proved by counting them, there were only fifty-two bottles—one for each week in the year—which was not enough anything like to cover the floor. Still, they made quite an impressive collection, neatly arranged in three rows across the room.

Philip picked up the bottle he had kicked over. It was quite small and obviously empty. "Medicine bottle," he remarked. He took the cork out and sniffed. "A pretty foul medicine too," he added.

"I suppose they're all the medicines Mrs. Worsley-Worsley had to have," Mary said. "I think she might have sent them for salvage, even if she was an invalid. But how beastly dull! I did hope we'd find something a bit more exciting, as a reward for all our exploring. Let's go downstairs again."

"We haven't looked in the box yet," said Philip hopefully.

"I bet it's got nothing in it," answered Mary. "Or if it has, it'll only be some more of those dismal bottles."

"I bet you sixpence it has," said Philip, more out of contradictiousness than anything else, and stepping warily across the floor, he reached the corner under the window.

The box was a very old leather trunk, covered in grey dust. There was no difficulty in opening it, for the lid was so perished with age that it came right away when Philip lifted it. He looked inside.

"Well?" asked Mary, who hadn't bothered to follow him down the room. "Who's won the bet?"

"I don't know exactly," replied Philip cautiously.

"What d'you mean?" Mary could tell from his voice that something was up. "You must know whether there's anything inside it or not," she added rather crossly.

"Well," said Philip slowly, "there's just one thing in-side it—a bottle."

"Oh! a *bottle!*"

"But it's quite a different sort to the others," Philip went on, and his voice sounded quite excited. "You'd better come and have a look at it, Mary."

Mary came down the room in such a hurry that she kicked over two medicine bottles and didn't bother to pick them up. By the time she had reached her brother he had already taken the bottle out of the box. Together they looked at it under the window.

It obviously was not a medicine bottle. For one thing it was much larger, and it was quite a different shape. It had a long, thin neck and bulged out below into a round, capacious body. There was no label on it and it had a cork in the top, kept in position by wire tied round the neck and secured by a seal.

"Do you think there's anything in it?" Mary asked.

"Sure to be," said Philip," or it wouldn't be corked like that. I don't know, though," he added. "It feels jolly light."

"Let's open it anyway," said Mary.

"I'm not sure if we ought to," Philip objected. He had rather painful recollections of undoing the wire on a bottle of cider which his father had left in the dining-room the Christmas before. The cork had come out by itself and a lot of the cider had come out with it, and what was worse the cider had turned out to be Mr. Jelf's very last bottle of champagne, worth untold gold, and the consequences had been terrible.

But while he was hesitating, Mary had already broken the seal and untwisted the wire. This time nothing happened. She took hold of the cork and gave it a tug.

"I can't move it," she complained.

Philip could not stand by and watch his sister struggling to do a man's work with her weak, girlish fingers.

"Let me," he said, and took the bottle from her.

The cork was certainly firmly wedged, and with all his strength at first he could not move it. Then he put the bottle on the floor and held it between his feet and pulled his hardest. Suddenly the cork came out with a loud "pop!" and before he could stop himself, Philip over-balanced and fell on his back.

When he recovered himself, the first thing he saw was

the bottle, lying on its side on the floor. He reached forward to pick it up, but Mary caught his arm.

"Look! Look!" she cried.

From the neck of the bottle was pouring, not liquid, but a stream of thick black smoke, which ascended in a cloud towards the roof of the low room and seemed to grow thicker and solider every minute.

"Gosh!" said Philip. "We've really done it this time!"

CHAPTER THREE

THE DJINN

★

The smoke, having risen nearly to the roof, did not spread about in the way that smoke usually does. Instead, it formed itself into a tall, dark column, not quite as high as the room itself, which wavered slightly from side to side in the draught from the open door. The smoke poured from the bottle in great puffs, and each puff straightway joined up with the main body, much as bees join a swarm when the queen has decided to settle somewhere. And just as a swarm will change itself in a few minutes from a flying cloud of insects into a compact, round ball that a brave man can shake off a tree into a box, so the column of smoke solidified itself, and took shape before their eyes.

The children watched open-mouthed. Long before the shape had taken its final form, while it was still blurred round the edges like a photograph taken with a camera that has wobbled, Philip realized what had happened, and he thanked his lucky stars that he had been reading *The Arabian Nights* that afternoon. Obviously, this was a Djinn, and Djinns, when they had been confined in bottles, were always extremely cross and very, very dangerous. Luckily, he knew now exactly what to do. All that was necessary was to persuade it to go back into the bottle before it could do any harm, and then, push the

cork in again as quickly as possible. The fisherman in *The Arabian Nights* had managed it quite easily and Philip was sure he could, too. After that the proper thing to do was to throw the bottle into the sea, but that might not be too easy. Even if going to the sea had not been out of the question these holidays, there would have certainly been awkward questions asked if he had wanted to take a large bottle in his luggage. However, there was a pond in the garden at Bolster Place, and perhaps that would do for the time being. The great thing was to be perfectly cool and not let him think that you were frightened.

It occurred to Philip that perhaps Mary *was* frightened. He remembered that she had not had the benefits of his education and had never read *The Arabian Nights*, except the story of Aladdin, which was of no use in the present crisis. He looked at her to see how she was taking it. So far as he could tell from her expression, Mary was more excited than frightened. Indeed, if anything, she seemed rather pleased. Her eyes were very large, her cheeks were pink and she was smiling and clapping her hands softly as though she was at the pantomime instead of being in mortal danger. Perhaps, Philip thought, there were advantages in being ignorant, so long as he was there with his superior knowledge to protect her.

"Three and a half minutes, exactly!" said a self-satisfied voice. "I think that's pretty good."

Philip looked round hastily at the column of smoke. But it was there no longer. In its place was a rather swarthy, dark-haired man in a neat dark brown suit, who was looking at his wrist-watch as he spoke. He did not look in the least like the Djinns in the illustrations in *The*

Arabian Nights, who were always at least ten feet high and had most alarming features. Philip was relieved to see that this one was of no more than ordinary size and had quite a good-natured expression. But that was no reason why he shouldn't be just as dangerous, he reflected, and he determined to remain on his guard.

"Considering we're allowed five minutes for the test," the Djinn went on, "I don't think I've done too badly."

Philip thought he saw his chance.

"Wouldn't you like to go back into the bottle?" he suggested, sounding as innocent as he could. "Just to see if you could beat your time?"

"Good gracious, No!" said the Djinn with a laugh. "Once is quite enough for me, thanks. Besides, I'm not trying for honours. A pass B.A. is as much as I want."

"What's a B.A.?" asked Mary.

"Bottled Afreet," the Djinn explained. "An Afreet is a special sort of Djinn, you know. We all have to pass the test to qualify."

Philip's blood ran cold, because anyone who has read *The Arabian Nights* knows that Afreets are the most dangerous sort of Djinns. And it didn't look as if this one was going to be so easy to get back into its bottle as the one in the story. Perhaps he had made a mistake in trying to be too clever, instead of sticking to the method laid down in the book. He decided to follow the fisherman's example.

"We've only got your word for it that you ever came out of the bottle," he said. "I mean, I wasn't really looking just now. Suppose you went back and did it again, then we should really know."

"Don't be silly, Philip," Mary put in. "Of course he came out of the bottle. I was watching every second of the time, if you weren't. And I thought he did it beautifully. Why on earth should he bother to do it all over again, just for you?"

Philip groaned. What was one to do with a sister who wouldn't even take the trouble to read *The Arabian Nights* and find out how to deal with an Afreet when you met one?

"For goodness' sake, shut up!" he whispered urgently, hoping the Djinn would not hear. "You don't understand a bit."

"What on earth are you talking about?" Mary whispered back. "I can't hear."

"Your brother is trying to explain," the Djinn interrupted, "that I am a highly dangerous creature, and the sooner I'm safely back in my bottle, the better. But as a manner of fact you needn't worry. If you look at the book again," he went on to Philip, "you'll see that Djinns only begin to be dangerous after they've been bottled a thousand years or so, and I haven't been anything like that time in here. In fact, I've had a very short spell indeed. Anyhow, all that Arabian Nights business is quite out of date. Mind you, I don't say that a Djinn really aged in bottle might not be a bit crusty, but nowadays we usually arrange matters to get decanted quite quickly and come out"—he smiled again—"quite sweet."

"I think you *are* sweet," cried Mary impulsively. "How did you get here?"

"That would be telling," the Djinn replied. "I think

it's my turn to ask a few questions, if you don't mind. To begin with, may I know your names?"

"Our surname is Jelf," said Philip. "I am Philip and this is Mary."

"Philip and Mary, eh?" said the Djinn. He did not go on to say, "You ought to be William and Mary," as strangers usually did, which was decidedly one up to him. Instead, he remarked, "Well, there was once a King and Queen called Philip and Mary, but Mary wasn't very popular and people have agreed to forget Philip altogether. Perhaps it's as well." And that might count as two up, being an out of the way piece of learning altogether.

"Now tell me," he went on, "to which of you do I owe the honour—I mean, which of you let me out?"

"Look here," said Philip, "if we tell you, is it really going to be all right? I mean, you're not going to play any Arabian Nights tricks on us?"

"Certainly not. I thought I had made that quite plain. On the contrary, the person responsible will, in the old phrase, hear of something to his—or her—advantage."

"Honest?" Philip persisted.

"Honest Afreet."

It sounded very impressive.

"Well then," said Philip, "we both did. I mean, I pulled the cork out actually, but it was Mary who undid the wire, and I should never have touched the cork at all if she hadn't done that first. So we were both in it."

"I see," said the Djinn. He stroked his chin and looked very thoughtful. "That makes it rather awkward."

"Why?" asked Mary.

"Well, the rules say that the person liberating a Djinn from his bottle is allowed a wish——"

"What sort of a wish?" asked Philip.

"Oh, the usual sort. Just an ordinary magic wish. But only one, that's the point. And you can't divide a wish very well. I mean, half a wish is no good to anyone. What ought we to do?"

The children looked at each other blankly for a moment. Philip knew quite well that the really noble thing for a brother to do in such circumstances was to offer the wish to his sister. But he knew equally well that he was not going to do anything of the sort. After all, he was the one who had really got the cork out with his own strong arm, which Mary could never have done alone. Besides, you couldn't trust a girl not to do something simply idiotic with a wish if she had it. He, on the other hand, would wish for something really useful—exactly what, he didn't know yet.

"You might toss for it," the Djinn suggested.

"That's a good idea," said Mary. "Have you any money on you, Philip?"

"No," said Philip. "Have you?"

"No," said Mary. "Djinn darling, could you lend us some?"

"Sorry," said the Djinn. "I never use the stuff." There was another pause.

"We could wish for some, I suppose," said Mary.

"Shut up!" cried Philip hastily. "If you're not careful you'll have wasted the wish before you know where you are."

Then Mary had a brainwave.

"Look here," she said to the Djinn. "If a grown-up opened the bottle and let you out, would he get a wish like anyone else?"

"Certainly. In fact it nearly always is a grown-up. They're much more in the habit of uncorking bottles than children, as a rule."

"Then those rules you were talking about are really meant for grown-up people?" Mary persisted.

"Yes, I suppose so," the Djinn admitted.

"Like tickets on trains and buses?"

"Like——? I don't quite know what you mean."

"I do," said Philip. "Mary, I think that's really bright of you. Look here, when Daddy takes the bus from Little Bolster to Bedstead Junction, he has to pay sixpence, because that's what the rules say the fare is. But if Mary and I go——"

"It's only threepence each," Mary put in. "Don't you see? Children half price. Well, why shouldn't it be the same for wishes? Two for the price of one?"

"That certainly sounds reasonable," said the Djinn. "Just let me see . . ."

There suddenly appeared in his hand, from nowhere, it seemed, a small paper covered book, on the outside of which was printed in large letters, "CONSOLIDATED REGULATIONS FOR DJINNS, PUBLISHED BY AUTHORITY. REVISED EDITION." He studied it carefully for some time.

"It doesn't say anything about children here at all," he announced at last.

"Oh!" groaned Philip and Mary together.

"So it looks as if we were free to make a new Regulation," the Djinn went on cheerfully.

He reached up to a rafter above his head and pulled down a cobweb, which he spread carefully on the open book in his hand. The cobweb immediately turned itself into a white piece of paper and became another page in the book.

"Useful things, cobwebs," observed the Djinn. He then wrote on the fresh page, using his finger as a pen.

"How will this do?" he asked, and handed the book to Philip.

Neatly printed on the page were the words: "*Regulation 18BA: WISHES, Djinns, for decanting: All children at half price.*"

"Lovely," said Philip.

Mary read it too, and then said doubtfully, "It looks all right, but is it solidified?"

"She means consolidated," Philip explained. "That's what the Regulations are supposed to be, aren't they?"

"Rather!" said the Djinn. "Solid, consolidated *and* solidified. Just try to tear it out."

Rather doubtfully, Philip pulled at the page, at first gently and then harder and harder. It remained firmly attached to the book and did not show the smallest sign of tearing. It was the solidest piece of paper you could imagine.

"That's all right then," said the Djinn, taking back the book, which immediately vanished in a small puff of smoke. "Now the only question to decide is—What do you want to wish for?"

CHAPTER FOUR

WISHING

★

After the Djinn said that, there was a long, long silence. It was so quiet in the room that they could distinctly hear Mr. Chaffers booming "Ah!" from somewhere far below, and, nearer at hand, the Djinn's wrist-watch ticking away the minutes while they thought and thought, and no idea came. It is awkward enough when an aunt or someone suddenly asks you what you would like for Christmas and the only things you can think of are either far too expensive for that particular aunt to afford, or else potty little objects which you could buy for yourself out of your Christmas tips, or even worse, something which you know would be considered "unsuitable". At least, Christmas comes round every year, and you can be practically certain that your aunt will think of something to give you, even if you can't. But a magic wish, the one and only you are ever likely to have in your life, is a much worse proposition. The very thought of wasting it was too appalling, and it drove every reasonable idea clean out of the children's heads.

"It *is* a bit difficult, isn't it?" said the Djinn, sympathetically.

"Dreadfully difficult," agreed Philip. "And we don't want to make a mess of it, like people are always doing in books."

"I think I'd like to wish for something quite simple," said Mary. "You know how Daddy is always complaining of being hard up? Well, why not just wish for an enormous lot of money?"

"The trouble is," said the Djinn, "that that's just about the least simple thing you can wish for nowadays. Of course it was different in the old times. If you found a lot of jewels and gold in a cave, like Ali Baba, you just hung on to it, and nobody bothered you with awkward questions. But if you did that now, you'd be worried out of your life. There was a man the other day who was given a wish, and he insisted on having a pot full of gold coins at the bottom of his garden. It was the kind that is always full of gold every morning, however much you have taken out the day before. Quite a useful thing to have about the place, you'd imagine. Well, it gave this poor fellow no end of trouble. You see, nobody is used to gold coins nowadays. He couldn't buy anything with them at the shops, and when he took them to his bank they were very severe with him and told him he could be prosecuted for hoarding. (He didn't say what kind of gold coins he wanted, so naturally we gave him oriental ones, which made it worse, apparently.) Then the Town Council of the place where he lived took over part of his land for allotments, and of course the very bit they chose was where his pot of gold was. After that, things really became impossible. Nobody ever found the gold—we always arrange that things of that sort will be invisible except to the owner—but naturally he wanted to visit it from time to time, and the people who worked the allotments couldn't make out why he was always trespassing on their ground. They thought he wanted to steal their brussels sprouts or something. In the end, after he'd been chased off by dogs three times and prosecuted for trespassing without lawful excuse twice, he gave it up as a bad job, and never went near his crock of gold again. No, wishing for money can have very awkward consequences."

"All right, then," said Philip. "Who wants gold coins, anyway? The proper thing to do with money is to put it into Savings. Everyone knows that. I think a fat lot of Savings Certificates would be a really good thing to wish for. A bit dull, perhaps, but nobody could make any difficulties about it."

The Djinn shook his head.

"I'm sorry to be so obstructive," he said, "but as a matter of fact, Savings Certificates would be even more awkward than gold coins. What would happen when you wanted to cash them? The Savings people would be sure to ask where they came from, and why they weren't recorded in their books, and all sorts of questions like that. You'd probably find yourselves had up for forgery or something before you knew where you were."

"Bother!" said Philip. Really, having a wish seemed to be almost more trouble than it was worth.

"Of course," the Djinn went on, "there are lots of other things to wish for besides money. For instance, you could wish for a pretty face or good manners——"

"Soppy!" said Mary disgustedly.

"—or courage, or honesty, or any good quality you like to think of."

"No," said Philip decidedly. "That would be cheating. I mean, you wouldn't feel a bit proud of not being frightened of anything if all the time you knew that it wasn't you really who was being brave, but simply that you were magicked into it. It would be like the invisible armour some chaps have in fairy stories, which always seems most unfair."

"Very true," said the Djinn.

There was another silence, during which Philip wondered whether he should not wish for a bicycle, only it seemed such a dreadful waste of magic. Then the Djinn spoke again.

"Well," he said, "we don't seem to be getting anywhere and we mustn't waste too much time, as I see that Mr. Chaffers has nearly finished his measuring and your grandmother will be calling for you directly." (How he could see anything of the kind was his own affair, but obviously he could.) "On the whole, I think the best plan will be for you each to have a suspended wish."

"What's that?" asked Mary.

"It simply means that you keep your wish up your sleeve, so to speak, for when it's needed. Then when you really want a bit of magic that will come in useful, you have only to wish and there it is."

"That sounds lovely," said Mary.

But Philip, who liked to think things out, was not so sure.

"I don't think that's a bit safe," he declared. "We should be sure to go and wish for something we didn't really want at all, and then be sorry for it afterwards. Suppose I was to say to Mary, 'I wish you'd shut up!' like I do sometimes, without thinking, the next thing I knew she *would* shut up, like an umbrella or a concertina, perhaps, and then never be able to open again. I'd be afraid to say anything to anybody if I had a wish hanging over me like that."

"No," said the Djinn reassuringly. "You needn't worry about that. I promise you that that sort of wish simply wouldn't count. Mind you, I don't say that the wish you do get may not come as a surprise to you. You might find you had wished for something without meaning to. But that will only make it all the more exciting. Whatever it is, it will be something you really want and something truly useful."

"I wish I could believe you," said Philip doubtfully.

"Don't you?" said the Djinn with a smile.

"N-no. Not absolutely. I'm sorry if I sound rude, but

I've read a lot about magic wishes, and there's nearly always a catch in them."

"Well," answered the Djinn, "You've just wished you did believe me, and you don't, so there's one wish that doesn't count, anyway."

"Oh . . .!" said Philip, and tried to work it out in his head. "I'll have to believe you, I suppose. That doesn't count as my wish coming true, does it?" he added anxiously.

"Not a bit. Your wish is still yours, to do what you like with." The Djinn looked at his watch. "We shall really have to look sharp," he went on. "Your grandmother will start calling for you in exactly one minute and a half from now. Is there anything else I can do for you?"

"Please," said Mary, "can I keep the bottle? It would look awfully nice on the nursery mantelpiece, and I should like to have it to remind me of you."

The Djinn looked rather doubtful. "We are supposed to return them all for salvage," he said. "There's a great shortage of Djinn-bottles just now. However," he added, apparently softened by Mary's pleading expression, "perhaps we could make an exception in this case."

He carefully corked the bottle and handed it to Mary

"Thank you ever so much," said Mary.

They were starting to go when Philip suddenly remembered a question he had been meaning to ask.

"What do Djinns do after they've taken their B.A.s?' he said.

"That depends. Personally, I'm going to Oxford and I think I shall become a famous Professor of something or other, I haven't decided what of yet. Most Djinns become famous men. Of course, they have advantages ordinary human beings haven't got."

"D'you mean," said Philip, "there are chaps going about looking like ordinary people who are really Djinns all the time?"

"Oh yes. And really, unless you knew how, you'd never tell the difference."

"It would be sickening to meet another Djinn and not know it," said Philip. "I wish I knew how to tell one when I saw him."

"Snap!" said the Djinn.

"I beg your pardon?"

"I said 'Snap!' You've wished a real wish this time, and you've had it."

"Look here!" Philip shouted, so angry that he was nearly crying. "That isn't fair! I only said I wished I knew, I didn't want to, really. I knew there would be a catch in it. And now I've gone and wasted my wish on a perfectly useless, measly thing that's no possible use to anybody! It's a rotten shame!"

"Nothing of the sort," said the Djinn in a very firm voice that made Philip quiet all at once. "You've got hold of about the most valuable thing you could possibly have. Next time you do meet a Djinn you'll know why. The reason why they make it so difficult to recognize them is . . ."

Philip and Mary found themselves alone in the empty room. The Djinn had vanished. They looked at each other in astonishment, wondering whether it had really happened, or whether they had been dreaming.

"Well!" said Philip at last.

"I wonder whether Granny really is calling for us," said Mary, going to the top of the back stairs.

Sure enough, she was.

Without saying another word, the two children ran downstairs and outside to where Mrs. Thwaites was waiting impatiently in the car.

CHAPTER FIVE

THE JELFS HAVE A VISITOR

*

"Whatever have you got there?" Mrs. Thwaites asked, when she saw the bottle in Mary's hand. It was rather an awkward question, Philip realized all at once, though when you came to think of it, it was not a very surprising one. After all, you could hardly expect to come out of the house with such an unusual object and not be asked what it was. And, although nothing whatever had been said between them on the subject, Mary must realize as well as he did that there were some things you simply could not begin to explain to grown-ups and this was one of them. All of which takes quite a lot of explaining, but actually took next to no time to pass through his rather agitated mind.

Mary's mind, however, did not seem in the least agitated, because she answered quite gaily, "It's a Djinn-bottle, Granny," as if it was the most ordinary thing in the world.

To Philip's immense relief, Mrs. Thwaites, too, seemed to take it in quite a matter-of-fact way.

"Rather an odd shape," she remarked casually, as she started the car. "Where did you find it?"

"In the box-room," said Philip. "There were lots of other bottles there—medicine bottles, mostly."

41

"Ah!" said Mr. Chaffers. "I'm not a bit surprised. That last nurse of Mrs. Worsley-Worsley's, she was a lot too partial to gin, if you ask me. I shouldn't wonder if you weren't to find quite a lot of empty bottles about the place. Nothing in it, I suppose?" he added hopefully.

"No," said Philip, and it was a great relief to be able to answer quite truthfully without giving anything away. "It's quite empty. Is it all right for us to keep it, Granny?" he added.

"Oh, yes! Certainly, if you want it," answered Mrs. Thwaites, and that was that.

"Philip," said Mary, as soon as they were alone together at home and the bottle was safely installed upstairs on the nursery mantelpiece, next door to the Noah's Ark, which they were much too big to play with now, "Philip, why on earth did you ask Granny if we could keep it? Suppose she had said, No?"

"Well, it was a risk," said Philip, "but after all, it was hers in a way. You see, she's bought Bolster Place, and I suppose that means everything inside the house. If it comes to that," he added thoughtfully, "she must have bought the Djinn as well, and we've sort of stolen him from her by letting him go. It would be rather a shock for her if she knew."

They both remained silent for some time, looking at the mantelpiece. There, in the familiar surroundings of the nursery, it seemed a very plain, matter-of-fact bottle, with quite an agreeable shape and a pleasant dark colour that gave out attractive greenish gleams where the light caught it, but without a hint of magic or anything extra-

42

ordinary about it. It might have been any old bottle, picked up anywhere. And suddenly all the excitement of the afternoon seemed to go flat, like the fizz in a glass of mineral water that has been left poured out too long.

"Philip," said Mary.

"What?"

"I suppose it did happen, didn't it?"

"Did what happen?" asked Philip.

"The Djinn and the wishes and everything."

"Must have," said Philip stoutly, though in his own heart he felt none too sure.

"You don't think we could have dreamt it or anything?"

Philip shook his head.

"Not unless we both dreamt the same thing at once," he said, "and I don't see how we could have done that."

"No, I don't suppose we could," said Mary, rather relieved, but she still looked doubtful, and went on staring at the bottle on the mantelpiece as if it could help her in some way. "Philip!" she said again, so suddenly that it made him jump.

"What?" said her brother, crossly. "I wish you wouldn't keep on shouting 'Philip!' at me like that. I'm here all the time, aren't I?"

"I've just thought of something," Mary went on. "If it really did happen, then you must have got your wish—about knowing Djinns when you meet them."

"Yes, of course."

"Well, then," said Mary, "how *do* you know a Djinn when he's not looking like one?"

43

Philip frowned fearfully in an effort to concentrate.

"I don't know," he admitted at last. "But perhaps I should remember if I met one," he added hopefully.

"I wish I was ten feet high!" exclaimed Mary in an angry voice.

Philip looked at her in alarm, but she remained exactly the same size so far as he could judge.

"You see?" Mary went on tearfully. "Your wish is no good and mine is no good. I believe the whole business is a sham, after all!"

Before Philip could say anything in reply, their mother came into the room. She was looking rather flustered and almost cross, which was unusual for her.

"Father has just got back from the City," she said. "He has brought a friend with him and they are going to be very busy talking business, so I want you to stay up here and go to bed as quietly as possible. I'll bring your suppers up in a minute."

"Isn't Daddy going to come up and say good night?" asked Mary.

"Mayn't we come down and say How do you do to the friend?" asked Philip.

"I don't think he wants to be bothered by children just now," Mrs. Jelf said, looking more flustered than ever. "He's a very busy man. But I dare say Daddy will come up and see you after he has gone."

"What's the friend's name?" said Philip. "Is it anyone we know?"

"It's nobody you know," his mother told him. "He is somebody Daddy met in the City, and his name is Sir Sigismund Kaufman-Fortescue."

"What a silly name!" cried Mary, and burst out laughing.

"Mary! Be quiet!" said Mrs. Jelf, looking quite alarmed. "He might hear you. Now please be good children and don't make a noise." And she hurried downstairs.

Sir Sigismund Kaufman-Fortescue, who was at that moment drinking sherry with Mr. Jelf in the sitting-room immediately below the nursery, was small and stout and flabby. He had a shiny bald top to his head, with just a rim of black hair surrounding it. Naturally, he was very rich. A man called Sigismund Kaufman-Fortescue simply couldn't help being rich, which was the reason why he had taken the name, although privately, like Mary, he thought it rather a silly one. He had tried being plain John Smith, but found that the only result was that he immediately began losing money, and as losing money was the one thing he positively detested, he decided to stick to Kaufman-Fortescue. He owned a large house not far away called Great Mattress, and he was on his way there from the City in his perfectly enormous car that afternoon when, happening to meet Mr. Jelf, he offered to give him a lift home.

Mr. Jelf was delighted at the chance of having a quiet talk to Sir Sigismund, because he was very much in need of his help at the time. Mr. Jelf was an inventor by profession, and very good at his job. He was continually inventing all sorts of highly ingenious gadgets, such as knitting-needles that counted the rows and stitches for themselves, or saucepans that turned into toasting-forks when required, and many other useful things of that nature. (Naturally Mrs. Jelf had all her husband's inventions in her house, but usually she forgot to use them, which was a sore point with him.) The trouble was that he found it a great deal easier to invent things than to persuade people to put up the money to manufacture them and advertize them and generally do all the expensive things necessary to turn them from beautiful ideas in Mr. Jelf's head into solid objects to be bought at any ironmonger's or household stores for good hard cash. As a result, in spite of all his cleverness, he had never yet succeeded in making much money.

He had just completed a particularly clever and complicated invention, which he called his masterpiece. He was perfectly certain that if only it could be put on the market it would make his fortune. But at the moment, for lack of money, the masterpiece simply consisted of a number of rather squiggly drawings on sheets of very creased paper, which he kept in a big envelope in his pocket, and was always prepared to show to anyone who might be interested. He had worked out that before the invention could be manufactured he would want just ten thousand pounds, which is a lot of money to a hard-working inventor, but of course a mere trifle to a man like Sir Sigismund.

Coming down from the city in Sir Sigismund's car, Mr. Jelf explained all about his invention and that if he would only lend him ten thousand pounds he would get it back in no time, because the invention was bound to be extremely successful and would sell at twenty-five shillings and elevenpence three-farthings (plus purchase-tax), whereas it would only cost sixpence halfpenny to make, once the machinery and things for making it had been paid for. Sir Sigismund was always very cautious about lending money, even small amounts like ten thousand pounds (which was another reason why he was so rich), but he was sufficiently interested to agree to come into Mr. Jelf's house and talk the matter over. And Mrs. Jelf could see from the look in her husband's eye that he intended to ask him to stay for dinner. That was what had made her flustered and almost cross, because of course there was next to nothing to eat in the house and Mrs. Marrable wasn't there to cook it.

Mrs. Jelf, however, was quite as clever an inventor as Mr. Jelf in her own way, and by the time Sir Sigismund had finished his second glass of sherry she had done something extremely ingenious with what was left of her very last packet of dried eggs and the remains of the Sunday joint, so that she was able to smile sweetly when Mr. Jelf casually invited his guest to stay and take what he called "pot luck". Only it was not luck at all but real ingenuity on the part of Mrs. Jelf.

Meanwhile, of course, there was also the children's supper to think of. They didn't get quite such pot luck as the guest, naturally, but there was just enough dried egg left in the packet to give them each sufficient scrambled egg to cover a big piece of toast, and in addition they had a mug full of cocoa apiece. Mrs. Jelf brought it up to them in the nursery on two small trays and then went downstairs to dish up dinner in the dining-room.

Sir Sigismund by this time had heard all about the invention several times over and he was beginning to

wonder whether it would not be worth while giving Mr.
Jelf ten thousand pounds at once to make him stop talking (much as the Jelfs used to give the waits sixpence at
Christmas to stop them starting up "Good King Wen-
ceslas" for the twentieth time); but when Mrs. Jelf opened
the door to announce that dinner was ready, such a rich
smell of food was wafted to his nostrils that he decided
to stay, instead of driving straight away to Great Mattress
as he had intended.

Philip and Mary meanwhile had been in the nursery,
listening to the burbling of voices from below and specu-
lating what it was all about. They felt rather hurt at
being exiled in this manner. Naturally they knew most
of their parents' friends and they were disappointed at
not being allowed so much as to have a look at this
one.

"I should think he's rather a pig, not wanting to
see us," said Mary, blowing at her cocoa which was very
hot.

"He might be anything with a comic name like that,"
said Philip, who was sitting on the floor, trying to balance
his tray on his knees. "Barely human, I should say."

Just then the burbling downstairs stopped for a moment and then they heard the sitting-room door open.

"He's coming out into the hall, I do believe!" exclaimed Philip. "Let's see if we can't have a squint at
him."

He got up, carrying his supper tray, and tiptoed
cautiously to the landing. Looking down the well of the
stairs he could see his father and mother and Sir Sigismund walking across the hall to the dining-room door.

Balancing the tray precariously on the edge of the banister rail, he leaned over to have a good look at the visitor.

It was impossible to get a clear view of his face, but the light of the hall lamp gleamed brilliantly on his shiny bald head. . . .

"Gosh!" exclaimed Philip in a loud, excited voice.

At that moment the mug of scalding hot cocoa, followed by the scrambled egg, slipped clean off the tray and descended in a cascade full on the top of Sir Sigismund's head.

CHAPTER SIX

SIR SIGISMUND'S SECRET

★

It is generally agreed among people who know such things, that if you want to borrow ten thousand pounds from anyone, you should take particular care not to allow hot cocoa and scrambled egg to be poured on his head. It has a very decidedly bad effect on business relations. If Mr. Jelf did not know it at the time, he learned it very shortly after, for although he and Mrs. Jelf did everything they possibly could to repair the damage, and indeed succeeded in mopping up all the cocoa and removing most of the egg-stains from Sir Sigismund's coat, there was nothing they could do to soothe his ruffled spirits. The more they apologized and tried to explain, the shorter his temper grew. He said several times and with growing emphasis that he had not come there to be made a fool of, and in the end he stumped out of the house in a fury, got into his huge car and drove away to Great Mattress.

It was a sad evening for the Jelf household. Mr. and Mrs. Jelf were left to eat her ingeniously invented dish alone, and found they had very little appetite for it. Philip's supper had all gone over the banisters on to Sir Sigismund's head, and in the circumstances he hardly dared to ask for any more, so he went to bed hungry. His father had told him that he would "see him in the morning" about his behaviour, so he had nothing very pleasant to look forward to. As for Mary, although nobody could say that what had happened was her fault, she was perfectly miserable at the way in which things had turned out. After the excitements of the afternoon there seemed to have been one disappointment after another, and she tossed and turned in her bed for a long time before she finally went to sleep.

Next morning, before he went to the City, Mr. Jelf "saw" Philip as he had said he would, but it turned out rather differently from what Philip had expected.

"I really don't know what to do with you, Philip," his father said. "In fact, I don't think there is anything I *can* do with you. If you had broken something worth sixpence I could stop it out of your pocket money. If you had done any ordinary kind of damage I could punish you in some way that would be more or less adequate. But when it's simply a question of depriving me of ten thousand pounds, what on earth can I do?"

"Ten thousand pounds!" said Philip. Of course, it was the first he had heard of it.

His father explained to him how Sir Sigismund had come to be in the house the previous night and what the effect of the accident with the supper tray had been. "And I simply cannot for the life of me imagine," he concluded, "how you came to be so appallingly careless. What on earth made you behave like that?"

"I—I really don't know," Philip muttered, turning red. "It just happened, I suppose. I'm awfully sorry."

"No doubt you are," said Mr. Jelf, who was inclined to get sarcastic when he was angry. "Unfortunately, your sorrow doesn't seem likely to be of very much practical use. Unless, by any chance you have ten thousand pounds saved up from your tips last Christmas which you could let me have?"

"No I haven't," said Philip, gravely. "But I will try to get it back for you, Daddy, honestly I will."

"That's a very fair offer," said his father, "and I'm sure I'm much obliged to you. Perhaps, if it is not asking too much, you could let me know how you propose to set about it?"

Philip hesitated, and opened his mouth to speak, but then thought better of it.

"Well?" said Mr. Jelf.

"Perhaps if I was to go and see Sir Sigismund," Philip said at last, "I could explain what happened and then he wouldn't be so cross—so cross with you, I mean," he added.

"Please don't try any such thing," said Mr. Jelf hastily. "You have done quite enough harm already, merely by looking at Sir Sigismund. Heaven knows what the effect would be of your trying to talk to him! I think, if you don't mind, you had better rest on your laurels. Well," he concluded, "I must be getting up to London, to see if there is anything to be done to put things right. But I'm very much afraid that it would take a cleverer inventor than I am to clear up the mess you have landed me in."

As soon as his father had gone, Philip ran off to find Mary. He found her in the nursery, trying to read a book and looking very dejected.

"What's happened?" she asked. "Was Daddy very angry with you?"

"He was a bit," Philip admitted. "But he's not going to do anything about it. He said that as I had lost him ten thousand pounds, there was nothing much he could do."

"I don't understand," said Mary. "I didn't know Daddy had ten thousand pounds."

"He hasn't," said Philip. "That's just the trouble." He explained what his father had told him, and went on, "I told him I'd get it back for him, but of course he wouldn't believe me."

"I should think not!" said Mary. "You know you couldn't do anything of the sort."

"Perhaps I couldn't, but you might, Mary. After all, you've still got the wish the Djinn gave you."

Mary shook her head.

"After what happened last night, I don't think I want to believe in Djinns at all," she said.

"After what happened last night," Philip retorted, "you'll jolly well have to."

"What do you mean?" asked Mary.

"I mean that Sir Sigismund is a Djinn himself, that's all."

"Sir Sigismund a Djinn!" said Mary. "But Philip, that's nonsense!"

"Why should it be nonsense?" said Philip.

"Well, because he's—he's just a person." Mary found it difficult to explain what she meant. "I mean, he didn't come out of a bottle or anything, but just came to the door in a car with Daddy."

"It wouldn't have made any difference if he'd come on a bicycle, or pushing a pram," said Philip. "He's a genuine, hundred per cent Bottled Afreet. That's why I dropped all my supper on his head."

"But why should you want to drop things on his head, just because he's a Djinn?" asked Mary, who was getting more and more puzzled.

"Silly! I didn't want to. That was just an accident, because I was so surprised and excited when I found out that I forgot all about the stupid old tray and over it went."

"But are you sure—about Sir Sigismund, I mean?"

"Absolutely sure," said Philip positively. "You remember I told you that I didn't know how I should be able to recognize a Djinn when I saw one, and until I saw Sir Sigismund I hadn't the vaguest idea how to do it. And then all of a sudden I remembered."

"You can't remember something if you didn't know it before," Mary objected.

"Can't you? It felt like remembering, anyway. Just as if I'd forgotten something that seeing him reminded me of."

"But you didn't even see him properly," said Mary. "I didn't, anyway. Only the top of his head before you poured all the cocoa on it."

"That was what made me remember," replied Philip. "The top of his head, I mean, not the cocoa, of course. When he came out into the hall the light was shining on it and in the middle of the bald piece I suddenly saw a funny little round dent. It was just the size and shape of the cork in that bottle." Philip nodded towards the mantelpiece.

"Well?" said Mary.

"Don't you see? When a Djinn's been shut up in a bottle, the cork must be pressing very hard on his head and that's what leaves the mark."

Mary remained unconvinced.

"I didn't see any mark on his head," she said. "And
had just as good a look as you did, even if I didn't spil
anything on him."

"I wish you'd stop talking about spilling things," said
Philip crossly. "You'd have done just the same if you'd
been me. And the reason why you couldn't see the marl
is pretty obvious, I should have thought. I had the wish
about recognizing Djinns and you hadn't. I dare say tha
mark's invisible to everyone in the world except me," he
added, rather proudly.

Mary said nothing for a moment. She was thinking
very hard and frowning horribly in the effort. Finally she
said, "If that's really right, and you weren't just imagin
ing things——"

"It's right enough," Philip interrupted. "I can't ex
plain it, but there was a sort of Djinnishness about tha
little hole on the top of his head——"

"*If* it's right," Mary repeated, "then it means that the
Djinn (our Djinn, I mean) was really telling the truth
about the wishes he gave us——"

"Of course he was!" said Philip excitedly. "And tha
means your wish is a good one, too. Don't you see, Mary
you can get Daddy his ten thousand pounds as easy
as—— Oh! I forgot," he added. "He said it was a
mistake to wish for money, didn't he?"

"Yes," Mary agreed. "Besides, I don't think Daddy
would really like it a bit if I was to give him ten thousand
pounds. He'd probably want to know where it came from."

"He'd be jolly well sure to," said Philip with emphasis
"He's most particular about money. Can you see us just
saying casually at breakfast one morning, 'Oh, Daddy,

56

here's a little present for you, with our love', and giving him all that money?"

"Tied up in tissue paper with a coloured ribbon," said Mary, giggling. "It would be an awfully big parcel, too. Just imagine Daddy's face!"

"No, Mary," Philip went on, "what we want to do is to get Sir Sigismund to lend it to Daddy just as he asked him to do last night. Couldn't you just wish him to do that?"

It was Mary's turn to look doubtful.

"Wouldn't that be wishing for money in a way?" she said. "Besides, if Sir Sigismund is a Djinn, himself, how do we know another Djinn's wish will work on him? Suppose he wishes not to?"

Philip scratched his head and looked at the floor as if he would find a solution for the problem there. Then he stared at the ceiling, but that didn't seem to give him any ideas either. Finally he fixed his gaze on the mantelpiece, where stood the bottle that had been the original cause of all the trouble.

"Let's think this out carefully," he said at last, addressing his words to the bottle rather than to Mary. "We want Sir Sigismund to come here and see Daddy again. Perhaps he'd come if you wished him to. I don't know, but we could try. But that would be no use if when he came he was still so cross that he didn't want to lend the money. The question is, how to make him not cross?"

Mary sighed.

"Oh, Philip, I wish everything wasn't so complicated!" she cried.

Before Philip could say anything, even to point out emphatically that this was *not* a wish that counted, the door opened and their mother came into the room. She looked rather harassed, but made no allusion to the sad events of the night before.

"Children," she said, "it's a lovely morning, and you ought to be out of doors. I think a walk would do you good. I want some things from the grocer's and I'm much too busy to go myself. Get your shoes on and I'll give you the list."

It was nearly a mile from the Jelf's house to the little village store where they did most of their shopping. Philip and Mary enjoyed the walk. After the rain of the day before the air was fresh and clear and the sun shone down from a cloudless sky. For the time being they forgot all about Sir Sigismund and all the troubles that he had caused. But no sooner were they arrived at their destination than they were forcibly reminded of him.

In the window of the shop was displayed a large poster, bearing the following words upon it, in heavy black type on a yellow ground:

BOLSTER RURAL DISTRICT COUNCIL ELECTIONS

PUBLIC MEETING

at the Memorial Hall, Eiderdown, September the 9th.

3 p.m.

Speaker:

SIR SIGISMUND KAUFMAN-FORTESCUE, B.A.
(Sleepers' Association Candidate)

Chairman:

FERDINAND FOLIOT-FOLJAMBE, ESQ., J.P.

Doors open 2.30 p.m.   All are welcome.

"September the 9th—that's to-day," remarked Mary.

"Yes," said Philip absently, as they passed into the shop. He said no more until, about two minutes later, while they were waiting to be served, he suddenly ejaculated, "Mary, I've got an idea!" so loudly and fiercely that the young lady assistant who was weighing out a purchase for another customer dropped what she was holding and sent about half a pound of best breakfast coffee flying all over the counter.

"Do you mean, how to make Sir Sigismund not cross?" Mary asked Philip in a whisper, under cover of the commotion caused by the coffee.

"Not exactly," was the reply. "I'll tell you when we get outside."

What Philip's idea was he explained to Mary on the way home, with the result that they arrived back at the house fairly sizzling with suppressed excitement.

CHAPTER SEVEN

STRANGE OCCURRENCE AT A MEETING

*

"What are you two thinking of doing this afternoon?" Mrs. Jelf asked at lunch. "Shall I ring
up Granny and ask if she is going over to
Bolster Place again?"

Philip tried to sound as casual as possible as he replied,
"Would it be all right if we took the bus into Eiderdown,
Mummy?"

"Eiderdown?" said Mrs. Jelf in surprise. "That's rather
a long way, isn't it? Nearly seven miles. Is there anything
special you want to do there?"

Philip went rather red.

"Oh well, I thought we might p'raps . . ." he muttered
and contrived to choke rather badly over his pudding.

"Well, I don't see why you shouldn't go if you want
to," said his mother, after the choke subsided. "It will be
something for you to do and I'm afraid these have been
rather dull holidays for you. If you take your ration cards,
you might see if you can get any chocolate there. There
doesn't seem to be any in Bolster."

Half an hour later two anxious figures might have been
seen waiting at the bus stop at the corner. Although it
was quite a warm afternoon, Philip was wearing his overcoat. It bulged considerably on one side and he kept his

arm up to prevent the round, rather slippery object beneath from falling. From time to time Mary murmured to him, "*Do* be careful of it, Philip!" and he whispered back, "Of course I will, silly!" They were both feeling rather nervous and not unnaturally this tended to make them cross.

The bus arrived. As it was market day in Eiderdown, it was crowded chiefly by large women with string bags, who took up a good deal of room. Philip and Mary squashed into a seat. At the next stop still more large women with bags got in and one of the largest of them trod on Philip's toes and muttered angrily that in *her* young days children were supposed to stand up for their elders. Philip was furious. He knew quite well he ought to stand up for ladies in buses, and the only reason why he did not do so on this occasion was that if he did the precious object beneath his coat would be certain to slip down if the bus gave a lurch. But of course he could do nothing about it, and had to endure the cross looks of the large woman all the way into Eiderdown.

They reached their destination as the clock in the market square pointed to ten minutes to three. Philip and Mary got out and found themselves in a crowd of eager shoppers who were clustering round the stalls which spread themselves all across the square. They stopped at one stall to buy a quarter of a pound of chocolate. Philip had some difficulty in getting the money and the ration card out of his pocket while still keeping one arm firmly across the bulge beneath his overcoat, which made the woman at the stall enquire rudely whether he'd got a baby in there. At the lower end of the square was the cattle market, and here the air was filled with the lowing of cows and the bleating of sheep and the pavement was crowded with red-faced farmers and dealers, most of whom looked as if they had eaten—and drunk—a good lunch. At the end of the square, overlooking the cattle market, was a tall, ugly building with the words " Memorial Hall" above the door, and towards this the children made their way.

"I hope we're not too late," murmured Mary as they pushed open the swing doors. "It's just three now, and the doors opened at half past two. Perhaps there won't be any room for us."

She need not have worried. Evidently the booths and stalls in the market place were a greater attraction to the people of Eiderdown than the Bolster Rural District Council elections. They followed a notice "To the Meeting" up a short stairway and then came into a large, draughty hall with rows and rows of hard chairs and at the further end a platform with a table in the middle of it.

On the table was a jug of water with a glass turned upside down on top. Immediately behind the water jug sat a tall, elderly gentleman with a melancholy downturned moustache. This was evidently Ferdinand Foliot Foljambe, Esq., J.P. On either side of him sat a number of other serious-faced men and women, also decidedly elderly. Most of them looked fairly drowsy, and one was certainly sound asleep. The children noticed immediately that Sir Sigismund was not on the platform. They noticed, too, that the chair immediately on Mr. F. F.'s right was empty. As to the body of the hall, that was nearly empty too. About a dozen people, not counting two babies in arms, were distributed among the rows of chairs. Among them Philip recognized the large woman with the string bag who had stood on his toes in the bus. She had evidently come to the meeting to rest her feet before going out into the market to fill the bag. Philip, who was of a forgiving nature, felt quite glad that she had found a seat somewhere at last. The hall was very warm and the windows looking out on to the square were open. Through them drifted the sound of the traffic, voices of the crowd and, above all, the noise of the livestock in the market, bellowing, grunting and bleating, according to their several natures.

Nobody took any notice of the children as they tip-toed their way up the hall and finally settled themselves on two chairs in the front row just under the chairman's table. But almost as soon as they had sat down, Mr. Foliot-Foljambe, as though he had been waiting for them, looked at his watch, coughed, rose to his feet and said in a loud voice, "Order, order!"

There was no reply to this observation, unless you could count a loud protesting squeal from a pig which was being lifted into a cart below.

"Ladies and gentlemen," Mr. Foliot-Foljambe went on, rather discomposed by the animal interruptions which punctuated his speech, "it gives me great pleasure (*Moo-oo-oo!*) to welcome you all to this meeting (*Grunt!*), and to see before me such a large and representative assembly (*Baa-aa-aa!*) of the Rural District electors."

At this point one of the babies began to cry very loudly, and Mr. Foliot-Foljambe had to stop. Mary took the opportunity to ask Philip, "What is a Rural District ejector?"

"Elector, not ejector," said Philip. "Ejectors are a sort of gun."

"Well, what is it, any way?"

"I've forgotten," said Philip, who never had known, but did not like to admit it. "But why isn't Sir Sigismund here?"

The baby was hushed to silence and the chairman began again.

"As you know," he went on, "this meeting has been called by that influential body, the Sleepers' Association."

Here the old gentleman who had been peacefully slumbering on the platform uttered a loud snore.

"Er—the Sleepers' Association," repeated Mr. Foliot-Foljambe, losing his way among the notes which he had spread out on the table in front of him.

The old gentleman snored again and there was a perfect chorus of baas and moos from beneath the window. Philip began to feel a bit sleepy himself. Whatever a Rural District elector was, he thought, it certainly was not a very exciting business. But he still kept his arm tight across his overcoat, and that kept him awake.

"We are looking forward to the privilege of an address from our candidate, Sir Sigismund Kaufman-Fortescue," proceeded the chairman, when he had found the right piece of paper at last.

"Hear, hear!" said a leathery-faced lady on the platform in a determined voice. She was echoed by a hen in the market which had just laid an egg while waiting to be sold and was cackling the news to the whole of Eider-down.

"Unfortunately," the speech went on, "Sir Sigismund has been delayed by important business, but we expect him with us at any moment. (*Baa-aa-aa!*) Meanwhile, until he does arrive, perhaps you will bear with me—"

At this point the woman from the bus got up and walked down the hall and out of the door at the far end. She had very squeaky shoes and made quite a commotion. The children felt sorry for Mr. Foliot-Foljambe, who was quite put out by this interruption, and Philip no longer regretted that he had not given up his seat to anyone so rude and inconsiderate.

"—bear with me," the harassed chairman repeated, "while I explain quite briefly the great importance of the forthcoming election."

"Hear, hear!" repeated the leathery lady, this time so loudly that she succeeded in waking up the old gentleman who had been snoring. He sat up, blinked, rubbed his eyes, and then, evidently not quite realizing where he was, ejaculated, "What are you doing, Clara?" which upset Mr. Foliot-Foljambe more than anything that had gone before.

None the less, in spite of all these difficulties, and in spite of the competition from the market-place, which never seemed to stop, Mr. Foliot-Foljambe did proceed to explain the importance of the election for ten minutes. To the children they were the longest ten minutes they had ever known. It was, Philip told himself, worse than the dullest sermon, because there was not even a hymn to look forward to at the end. But at last, when the chairman was in the middle of a very long and involved sentence, a loud, imperious hoot from a motor-horn was heard just outside. Mr. Foliot-Foljambe stopped abruptly, craned his neck to look out of the window, and then abandoning his speech with every sign of relief, said, "Ladies and gentlemen, our candidate has arrived!"

A moment later, Sir Sigismund came into the hall and walked up the platform with hurried strides. Everybody, led by the chairman, clapped their hands, except for the babies, of whom one was asleep and the other set up a mournful wail. The combined noise echoed rather dismally in the nearly empty hall, but Sir Sigismund did not seem in the least discomposed. He climbed quickly on to the platform, shook hands with the chairman and took his seat with an expansive smile.

Mr. Foliot-Foljambe turned to the audience once more.

"And now ladies and gentlemen," he said, "I have very much pleasure in introducing to you Sir Sigismund Kaufman-Fortescue!"

Sir Sigismund, who was dressed in a very gay suit of check tweeds and had a large carnation in his buttonhole, rose to his feet.

"Now's the time!" whispered Philip to Mary, and she nodded, her eyes bright with excitement.

From beneath his overcoat he produced the Djinn bottle, silently removed the cork, and set it up against the foot of the platform, just beneath where Sir Sigismund was standing.

"Mr. Chairman, Ladies and Gentlemen!" Sir Sigismund began in a clear, confident voice. At the same time,

Mary, leaning forward in her chair, and speaking in low but distinct tones, uttered these fateful words:

"I wish that Sir Sigismund Kaufman-Fortescue should turn back into smoke and come into this bottle!"

Then the children sat back in their chairs and watched the platform to see the result.

For a few dreadful moments it looked as if nothing was going to happen. Sir Sigismund continued with his speech. "I must begin by apologising," he said easily, "for my late arrival here, which is due to . . ."

He paused and looked down at his feet. An uneasy expression came over his face. As he did so, the children, from their seats below the platform, saw a thin trickle of black vapour oozing through the cracks between the planks of the platform. It formed itself into a narrow column and first slowly, then with increasing rapidity, poured itself into the neck of the bottle.

"Er—due to important public engagements elsewhere," said Sir Sigismund in rather faltering tones, still manfully trying to continue with his speech under what must be admitted to have been rather exceptional difficulties. By now, not only his feet but his legs up to the knees had dissolved into smoke and were being sucked remorselessly into the bottle. His head and the upper part of his body still looked solid enough, but it was apparent that they had no firm support, and only by keeping a firm grip on the table with his hands did he save what was left of himself from dropping to the floor.

To the children, even though they knew what was happening, it was a fascinating spectacle, more exciting in its way than when they had opened the bottle for the first time. Nobody else, of course, had any idea of what was going on, and the table hid the lower part of Sir Sigismund (or rather the place where it should have been) from the view of most of the audience. But both Mr Foliot-Foljambe and the leathery-faced lady (who sat on either side of him) looked at what they could see of their candidate in some alarm.

"I shall not detain you long," declared Sir Sigismund in a last despairing effort. And indeed he did not. For the magic at this point decided to act quickly, as though it were dissatisfied with the slow progress up to this point. The rest of Sir Sigismund disappeared quite suddenly. It was almost like blowing out the flame of a candle. At one moment there was the upper part of his gay suit, the waistcoat buttons strained by the ample chest and

68

stomach inside, and on top of it his broad, heavy face with its double chin; the next, there was nothing but a cloud of black smoke, which poured with astonishing speed downwards to the floor of the platform and from

there into the bottle waiting to receive it. In the space of a few seconds the place on the platform next to Mr. Foliot-Foljambe was completely empty, while in the front row of the seats below Philip triumphantly rammed home the cork.

For a moment there was complete silence in the hall, against which the animal noises outside sounded louder than ever. Then everybody began to talk at once. Everyone on the platform stood up, except for the chairman and the leathery-faced lady, who simultaneously went down on their knees to see whether Sir Sigismund was hiding under the table, and bumped their heads together very hard in the process. The people at the back of the hall, more awake now than they had been at any time since the meeting began, charged forward towards the platform in a body. Very soon the whole meeting was crowded round the place where Sir Sigismund had been, arguing and disputing at the top of their voices.

"We must send for the police!" said the leathery-faced lady, with her hat all askew from the bump that the chairman had given her.

"You don't want the police, lady, you want the fire-brigade," said a man from the back of the hall. "He set fire to himself, that's what. Didn't you see the smoke?"

"Where's the funny man gone to, Mummy?" asked a little girl in a shrill voice. "I want to see the funny man again!"

"But he must be somewhere about!" said Mr. Foliot-Foljambe helplessly. "I saw him here only a moment ago, with my own eyes! Look, some of you, look for him!"

And look they did, under chairs and behind curtains, even behind the large bust of Queen Victoria which stood on a shelf at the back of the platform. They looked everywhere. Everywhere, that is, except in the bottle, which, with its precious contents, was now safely ensconced once more beneath Philip's overcoat.

Over the din of voices, Mary heard the chime of the clock in the market square.

"Philip," she said, "that's half past three. If we hurry now, we can just catch the bus home."

"Come on," said Philip.

Nobody in the hall noticed the two children as, flushed with triumph, they slipped out, carrying with them the hapless candidate for the Bolster Rural District Elections.

CHAPTER EIGHT

WHAT HAPPENED ON THE WAY HOME

★

"We've got Sir Sigismund! We've got Sir Sigismund!" chanted Mary in her excitement as she and Philip raced down the stairs of the Memorial Hall and into the square. "Philip, hasn't everything gone simply marvellously! Now, all we have to do is to get him home and——"

"He'll simply have to do what we want when we let him out of the bottle," said Philip. "We shan't have any doubt about what to wish for this time, shall we, Mary?"

"But don't forget there will be a wish to spare," Mary reminded him. "Children half price. That's a solidified regulation, isn't it?"

"Rather!" said Philip, happily. "And now we know how to do it, what's to stop us going about catching Djinns whenever we see them and charging two wishes every time we let them out? Gosh! What a lark it would be! There's a chap at school who spends all the hols. catching butterflies. It would make him stare a bit if I told him I'd spent mine catching Djinns!"

The idea tickled his fancy so much that he had to stop and laugh out loud.

"We'll have to hurry," said Mary. "Look, there's the

bus just coming up to the stop, and there's a beastly long queue already."

Running across the square and dodging between the market stalls, they reached the end of the queue just as the bus drew up. Philip could see at once that it would be touch and go whether or not there would be room for them by the time all the people in front had got in. The passengers took longer to fit themselves into the bus than it had taken Sir Sigismund to get into the bottle, and by the time the children reached the head of the queue, more people had attached themselves to its tail. It was obvious that most of these would be disappointed, and presently there was some ugly jostling and pushing from behind.

"Room for one more only!" cried the conductress, just as Philip was about to put his foot on the step.

Philip hesitated for a moment. Did he and Mary count as one? They did for magic wishes, he knew, but for the moment he had forgotten the rules for buses. The hesitation was fatal. The next instant he was violently pushed on one side and his old enemy, the fat lady with the string bag, charged past him on to the bus. It was so unexpected that Philip was nearly knocked off his feet. His arm flew up and the precious bottle, slipping from under his coat, went crashing to the ground.

To the children's astonishment, it did not break. Instead it did something far more remarkable and, as it turned out, very nearly as troublesome. It bounced. And it was no mere straight up and down bounce either, like a tennis ball that has been dropped directly on to the ground. This was a sideways bounce, at an acute angle, astonishingly long and low considering what a short distance it had fallen in the first place. In fact, as Philip said afterwards, it was really more like flying than bouncing—as though the bottle knew where it was going. And the flight ended plump in the middle of a stall of second-hand glass and crockery several yards away. There the bottle landed, neatly and quietly, without disturbing any of the other goods on the stall, and sat up on its base as though it had been there all its life.

The children had noticed that particular stall when they came through the square on their way to the meeting. It was full of rather unattractive oddments—chipped glasses and cracked jugs, saucers that had lost their cups and cups that had lost their handles and things of that nature. But what had especially attracted their attention was the stall-keeper. They had noticed him because he looked so different from all the other buyers and sellers in the market. He was a dark-skinned little man, with coal-black, frizzy hair and light brown eyes. In the lobes of his ears were small gold rings, and he had a large turquoise and silver pin in his necktie. He never kept still for a moment, but waved his brown hands about incessantly, all the while jabbering to the crowd in a strange accent.

Philip and Mary ran as fast as they could to the stall where their bottle sat, between a cracked bedroom ewer and a decanter without a stopper. There was no crowd round the stall now, and the dark man was just beginning to pack up his wares to go home.

"Please," said Philip, all out of breath, "can we have our bottle?"

"Your bottle, eh?" said the man. "And what do you mean, your bottle, please?" (He pronounced it pleasse, with a lot of s's in it.)

"This one, of course," said Mary, reaching up her hand to take it. But before she could touch it, the man had

picked it up and stood holding it by the neck in his dirty hand.

"Oh, thiss one, iss it?" he said. "Forgive me, pleasse, but I did not remember that you have bought it."

"Of course we haven't bought it," said Philip. "It's ours."

The man looked at him with those very disturbing light brown eyes.

"If you have not bought it, how iss it yourss, pleasse?" he asked, still keeping hold of the bottle.

"But it is ours," Philip persisted.

"You know it isn't yours, anyway," Mary added.

"But if it iss not mine, young lady," said the man, "what iss it doing on my stall? Can you tell me that, pleasse?"

"Well, it just came here," said Philip. "I dropped it, and—— But you must have seen it yourself."

"Indeed, young sir, but I never saw any such thing," the man answered with a horrible grin. "And bottless don't come on my stall by themselves, nor jugss, nor saucerss. And nothing comess off my stall either, unless it iss properly paid for." He held the bottle up to the light in one hand and stroked it lovingly with the other. "And this bottle iss vairy, vairy expensive, I think."

"But look here——!" Philip began hotly and then stopped. What on earth was he to say or do?

"You were saying, pleasse?" said the man grinning more horribly than ever. He was still holding the bottle out of the children's reach, gazing at it, as though he could see what was inside.

At that moment a large red hand suddenly reached across the stall and closed on the stall-keeper's thin brown wrist, and a loud, rough voice exclaimed, "Now then, you 'eathen devil, you 'and over that there bottle!"

The children looked round, and saw a tall, shabbily dressed man, with a rather coarse, red face and a very truculent expression.

"You let go my hand, pleasse, this instant!" cried the

brown man, trying to wriggle away. He was no longer grinning, but looked very savage. "You let go my hand, I tell you, or I call the police!"

"Call the police indeed! That's what I've half a mind to do!" said the newcomer. "I know your dirty tricks, you thieving varmint!"

And with a quick twist of his powerful hand he wrested the bottle from the stall-keeper.

"Here you are, my little lady," he said to Mary, handing it to her with a rather unsteady bow. "Here's your propputy, safe an' sound." His little speech ended with a loud hiccup, which rather spoiled the effect.

"Thanks awfully!" said Philip, quite overcome with gratitude at having been helped out of such an awkward situation.

"That's quite all right——" the man began, but he was interrupted before he could say more by the stall-keeper. He no longer looked savage or frightened. Instead, he had all at once become extremely humble and submissive.

"Oh pleasse, young sir and young lady!" he began, twisting his hands together in supplication. "You will let me have this bottle, will you not? Look, I give you plenty moch money for him—all the money you want! He iss vairy, vairy fonny bottle, but not good for young lady and gentleman. Listen pleasse, I am only poor man, but I give ten shillings for him. . . ."

Philip and Mary thought he was even more disgusting talking in this new style than he had been when he imagined he had succeeded in stealing the bottle. They turned away as quickly as they could.

"I give you five pounds for him!" he shouted after them. "I give you twenty pounds, I say!" And then, as they still walked away, he called out some angry words in a foreign language which they did not understand. It might have been only her imagination, but Mary, who was holding the bottle, thought that at the sound of them the bottle itself began to squirm in her hand. It was an uncanny feeling, and she gripped it as firmly as she possibly could.

"What are we going to do now?" said Philip, as soon as they were out of earshot of the stall. "There isn't another bus to Bolster for half an hour, and we can't hang about here till then. That brute would only have another shot at pinching the bottle, for certain."

"You going Bolster way?" said their new acquaintance, who was still close beside them. "Let me give you a lift in my car." (He ran his words together in a rather curious way, so that what he said sounded like "Lemmegivyerliftimmecar," but Philip was able to understand his meaning.)

"It's awfully kind of you," said Philip doubtfully. He was not at all sure that this was exactly the kind of person his parents would wish him and Mary to accept lifts from. At the same time, after what had happened, he was anxious not to say anything that could hurt his feelings. It was Mary who decided him.

"Oh, Philip, do let's!" she said. "We promised Mummy to be home to tea, and"—she whispered—"we don't want Sir Sigismund to get cross by being shut up any longer than he has to be."

Philip nodded and turned to the stranger.

"We should like to come very much," he said. "If you're sure it's not giving you too much trouble."

"You're welcome," was the reply. "All on me way ome. C'm on. She's just round the corner."

He led the way to a side street, where a small, shabby car was standing. It was very dirty, and the back seats were crowded with such a variety of objects, wrapped and unwrapped, that the children wondered where they should find room for themselves. But by dint of clearing some of them on to the front seat and heaping others on the floor, the man made just enough space for them, and Philip and Mary wedged themselves in, between a sack of chicken food and an old and rather smelly horse rug. After all that had happened that afternoon, they suddenly began to feel very tired. They leaned back on the hard leather cushions and looked at each other with a reassuring smile. Everything was going right after all! Mary put the bottle on the floor between her feet for safety.

"It's all right, Sir Sigismund," she said softly to it. "We shan't keep you shut up long."

After several attempts, the car started with a roar and a rattle, and they drove out rather jerkily into the main street. There was a good deal of traffic about, including some bewildered cattle which had been sold in the market and were being driven away by their new owners. But their driver seemed to think that everything else on the road, whether it went on wheels or on two legs or four, ought to get out of his way. He kept his thumb pressed on the electric horn and fairly ploughed his way through. Several times it looked as though there must be an accident, but somehow he just managed to avoid disaster.

The Jelfs had no car of their own, but Philip knew enough about cars to feel that this was not the way to behave on a crowded road. His grandmother, for instance certainly never drove in that fashion. And when other people on the road annoyed her by driving too close or turning suddenly without giving a warning, she would sometimes murmur uncomplimentary remarks about them beneath her breath, but she never, like this driver leant out of the window to roar abusive words at them as she passed. Philip felt quite ashamed to be driven in such a manner, and he was thankful when they were clear of the crowds and out in the open road.

The driver, too, seemed pleased to find himself out of the town—so pleased, in fact, that he began to sing in a hoarse, throaty voice. At the same time, he increased speed, so that the little car fairly flew along, bumping over the rough places and swaying from side to side at every bend in the road. The children found themselves hanging on to the sack of chicken food, or anything else available, to avoid being thrown from their seats as they lurched round the corners, of which there were many between Eiderdown and Little Bolster. It began to be quite alarming. Mary called to him to go more slowly but between the noise of the car and his own singing he evidently could not hear her, for he only went the faster

"Oh, Philip, I wish he wouldn't go so fast. I'm frigh tened," said Mary to her brother, when she saw that she could do nothing to check the furious speed of the car.

"It's all right," said Philip reassuringly, though he fel anything but comfortable himself. "We're nearly home now. That was Featherbed we have just come through

and we shall be at Bolster Place in a minute. Mummy'll
be surprised to find us back so soon."

They flashed past Bolster Place so fast that they had
no time for more than a glimpse of the kitchen garden
wall and missed the sun-dial altogether. After that they
had to ascend a long slope, from the top of which the road
ran gently down into Little Bolster village. At the crest of
the slope was a bend in the road, and the car went round

it as it had done all the other bends since Eiderdown,
the engine roaring, the wheels screaming and the driver
singing at the top of his voice. They had rounded the
bend and started to come down the hill when the children saw that just in front of them was an elderly man on
a bicycle, free-wheeling slowly down in the same direction. Apparently the noise of their approach startled him,
for he looked over his shoulder. Then they recognized
Mr. Chaffers. Evidently he was on his way home from
Bolster Place. The two-foot rule was sticking out of his
coat pocket and he was carrying a bag of tools in one hand
and guiding the bicycle with the other. Whether it was

the weight of the bag, or the result of looking round, or the fright that the noise of the car had given him, or all three put together, it was impossible to say, but the bicycle suddenly began to wobble most alarmingly and strayed towards the middle of the road. The next moment they were right on top of him. The car swerved frantically, but it was going much too fast to avoid him. The front of the car charged straight into Mr. Chaffer's back wheel with a hideous "Crash!" The children had a fleeting glimpse of the poor old man flying through the air in one direction, his bag of tools in the other, while the car plunged onwards down the slope towards the village as fast as ever.

"Stop! Stop!" the children shouted together. But at first it did not seem as if the driver intended to stop. It was only when Mary pommelled him on his back and shoulders and screamed in his ear, "You've knocked poor Mr. Chaffers down! You *must* stop!" that he took any notice. Then he put on his brakes and the car slithered to a stop a good hundred yards beyond where the bicycle lay, badly damaged, in the middle of the road.

The driver seemed in a very bad temper, as if what had happened was anybody's fault but his own.

"Thiswotcomesotryintoelpeople," he muttered, running his words together more than ever. "'Seeafriendoyours?" he added, jerking his thumb over his shoulder.

"Of course he's a friend of ours," said Philip indignantly. "It's Mr. Chaffers."

"Youbessgobackanseewotsappend," suggested the man, and leaning back in his seat he opened the door of the car for them. But he did not make any move to get out himself.

Philip and Mary did not need any further prompting. They jumped out at once and ran back up the road as fast as their legs would carry them.

They found Mr. Chaffers sitting disconsolately at the side of the road, with his feet in the ditch. They were relieved to find that he did not appear to be seriously injured. He had been thrown into the hedge, which had broken his fall, but he was badly scratched and bruised, and he was, not unnaturally, very, very angry indeed. When they came up to him, he was picking thorns out of himself and uttering rude noises under his breath. He could hardly believe his eyes when he recognized the children.

"Well, fancy seeing you two!" he exclaimed. "Where do you spring from?"

"We were in the car," panted Philip, all out of breath from his run up the hill. "Oh, Mr. Chaffers, I *am* sorry——"

"In the car!" Mr. Chaffers was so surprised that he forgot his injuries for a moment. "How did you come to be with a fellow like that? Why, he must have been drunk the way he was driving!"

"He gave us a lift from Eiderdown because we couldn't get on the bus," Mary explained.

Philip said thoughtfully, "Yes. I think he must have been drinking. That would explain a lot of things."

"And why didn't he stop when he saw what he'd done?" Mr. Chaffers went on wrathfully.

"He did stop when we told him to," said Mary. "He's just half-way down the hill now, and we ran back to see if we could help."

Mr. Chaffers with a groan got stiffly to his feet and looked down the road.

"He ought to have come back hisself," he muttered, and then exclaimed angrily, "Look at him now, the brute!"

The children looked too. The car was no longer where they had left it. Instead, it was moving slowly away, down the hill. As they watched, it gathered speed, turned the corner at the bottom and in a moment was lost to sight.

"Gosh! That's pretty cool!" said Philip disgustedly. "To run away like that after an accident———"

He was interrupted by a cry from Mary.

"Philip! Sir Sigismund! The bottle's still in the car!"

The children looked at each other in silent horror. For a moment they forgot all about Mr. Chaffers and his troubles. They were conscious only of one thing—that Sir Sigismund Kaufman-Fortescue, on whom all their hopes depended, turned into smoke and corked up in a bottle, was being driven further and further away from them by a drunken man whose name they did not know, to a destination they could not guess.

CHAPTER NINE

AFTER THE ACCIDENT

★

'Did you get his number?" said Mr. Chaffers anxiously, still gazing after the vanished car.

Philip shook his head. He was too over-whelmed by the disaster that had happened to trust himself to speak.

"Ought to have had his number," Mr. Chaffers grumbled. "This is a job for the police, this is. Drunk in charge of a car, dangerous driving, failing to stop after an accident—I'll have him shut up! And my damages, too—just look at my poor old bike!"

He hobbled out into the road and picked up his damaged bicycle. The back wheel was smashed to pieces, and the handle-bars were bent all out of shape. He carried it to the side of the road and then began to look for his tools, which were scattered all over the place.

"Ah!" he exclaimed suddenly, almost with a touch of his old manner. "Of course, I'd forgot, you were in the car with him, weren't you? What's his name?"

"We don't know," said Philip miserably.

"Well, you know where he lives, for sure. We can trace him quick enough that way."

"But we don't know even that," Philip told him. "He just said Little Bolster was on his way home and offered to give us a lift. I wish to goodness we'd never taken it."

"That's bad, that's bad. But there's no need for you to upset yourselves about it," said Mr. Chaffers in a kindly tone, seeing that both children were near to tears. "Nobody can say it was any fault of yours. Thank'ye, my dear," he added to Mary, who had just handed him his cap which she had discovered in the ditch. "And I reckon I ought to be glad you two were there," he went on. "You'll be a fine pair of witnesses for me if I bring this case to Court—that is, if you wouldn't mind coming and speaking for me when we catch this fellow?"

"Of course we wouldn't," Mary answered him. "It isn't that that's worrying us. You see, we left something of ours in the car and he's gone off with it."

"Oh, so he's a thief as well, the dirty vagabond!" said Mr. Chaffers.

Philip felt that he must be fair, even to a man who had caused so much trouble.

"Well, he hasn't stolen it exactly," he said. "I don't think he knows it's there, actually. But it's frightfully important and we simply must get it back."

"Ah!" said Mr. Chaffers. "Is that my spirit level lying over there? Perhaps you'd pick it up for me, it hurts me to stoop after hitting the hedge so hard with my back. Thank ye, I'm much obliged. And what was it, exactly you'd left in that ruffian's car?"

Philip hesitated, but Mary said at one, "It was a bottle. The one we found at Bolster Place yesterday."

"Ah," said Mr. Chaffers. "I remember. What did you want to go trapesing about to Eiderdown with that for?"

This was something the children felt they could no

86

possibly answer, but luckily Mr. Chaffers did not pursue the subject. Instead, with their help, he set about retrieving all the tools that had fallen from his bag, and it was not long before they had been reassembled. They were little the worse for wear except for a small handsaw, the teeth of which had suffered from falling on the road. Mr. Chaffers grieved over this even more than he had done over his bicycle and murmured "Ah!" as he looked at it in a deep, fierce tone that boded ill for the wrongdoer when he should lay hands on him.

When this had been done, they set off to the village. Mr. Chaffers, who was limping very badly, insisted on carrying his wrecked machine, while Philip and Mary managed the heavy bag of tools between them. This made their progress very slow, and it was lucky that the police station, where Mr. Chaffers wished to call first, was at the near end of the village. The police sergeant to whom he spoke was extremely sympathetic and was hopeful of tracing the car driver before long.

"The car must have been damaged in the collision," he said. "I'll notify my headquarters and they'll have a sharp look out kept for any car that looks as if it's been in an accident lately." He turned to the children. "You'd recognize this man if you saw him again?" he asked.

"Yes!" Philip and Mary said together.

"Good! I daresay we shall be sending along for you to identify him one of these days. He sounds as if he might be one of those chicken farmers up Bedstead way. If so, we'll pull him in, never fear."

"Philip," said Mary as they left the police-station, where they had left Mr. Chaffers still conferring with the sergeant, "you never said anything to him about the bottle."

"I know I didn't," said Philip gloomily. "What earthly good would it have been? He'd not have been a bit interested in an old bottle left behind in the car, and if we'd told him what was inside it, he would simply not have believed us."

Mary tried to imagine what it would be like trying to explain to a policeman that Sir Sigismund Kaufman-Fortescue was cooped up in a bottle in the back of a ramshackle motor-car, along with a sack of chicken food and an old horse rug, and she had to agree that it was impossible.

"I do feel horribly tired," she said. "I wish home wasn't the other side of the village. I seem to have walked miles and miles to-day."

"We might pick up a bus at the Seven Sleepers," Philip said. (The Seven Sleepers was the name of the village inn.) "That would save our legs the last bit of the way, at least. It ought to be due about now. Let's hurry, Mary, in case it passes us before we get there."

Hardly were the words out of his mouth, however, when with a loud "Honk!" the bus from Eiderdown sailed round the corner behind them and swept past to the stopping place at the Seven Sleepers two hundred yards further on, without taking any notice of their frantic waving.

"Blow!" said Philip. "That's torn it! There won't be another one for half an hour at least, so we shall just have to walk the rest of the way. What's the matter, Mary?"

Mary had gone quite pale and was staring after the disappearing bus.

"Didn't you see?" she said. "He was in the bus!"

"Who was in the bus? Our car-driver, do you mean?"

"No, of course not," said Mary impatiently. "That horrid brown man in the Market."

"Good Lord!" said Philip. "Are you sure?"

"Of course I am. You know my eyes are—are pretty good," said Mary. She did not want to hurt Philip's feelings by reminding him how much sharper her sight was than his.

"Do you think he noticed us?" Philip asked.

"Must have, I should think. He was looking out of the window on our side and the bus came close past us. Oh, Philip, do you think he's come after the bottle?"

"Well," said Philip with a dismal attempt at humour, "if he knows where the bottle is, he knows more than we do, that's all."

"He did seem frightfully keen on it," said Mary. "Almost as if he knew what sort of a bottle it was. Do you think he could be a Djinn, too?"

"No," said Philip with emphasis. "He isn't. I'm sick of Djinns, anyway," he added.

They walked on for some way in silence.

"I wish to goodness you hadn't left the bottle behind when you got out of the car," Philip said at last.

"I like that!" Mary answered crossly. "It was you just as much as me. You'd been carrying it about all day, hadn't you?"

"Well anyhow," Philip retorted, "it was your idea taking a lift in that rotten car. That was what made all the trouble."

"I couldn't tell he was going to knock down Mr. Chaffers and then run away, could I?" said Mary indignantly. "He seemed quite friendly at the Market."

"Well, it's no use arguing about it," said Philip. "It was both our faults, really. I suppose he ran away because he was scared when he saw what he had done. Especially if he was a bit drunk."

"Perhaps when he gets over being drunk he'll bring the bottle back," said Mary. "After all, he knows it's ours."

"Much more likely to open it, I should think," replied Philip. "It'll give him a bit of a shock when he does, won't it? And Sir Sigismund, too," he added with a laugh.

"Oh, don't, Philip!" Mary protested. "It's much too serious to make jokes about."

"I know it is," said Philip soberly, and they trudged on for some way without speaking.

"I've just thought of something," Mary observed, as their house came into view. "How much are we going to tell Mummy?"

"Nothing about the bottle," said Philip decisively. "That would be absolutely fatal."

"No," Mary agreed, "not about the bottle. But about the car and the accident and everything. After all, Mr. Chaffers is bound to tell Granny and then Granny will tell Mummy."

"You can never be sure what Granny will or won't do," said Philip. "Good old H.M.S. Unpredictable!"

"But she may tell her," Mary persisted. "And anyway, f we have the police calling about the man in the car, hen everything's bound to come out."

"And then there'll be a row," remarked Philip philo-ophically. "Daddy will say we've been—what does he :all it?—secretive, which always annoys him. Well, I :an't help that. We are being secretive anyway, and here'd be a much bigger row if he knew what had really 1appened."

"But what are we going to say if Mummy asks us why ve're so late?" Mary said.

"Well, then we shall have to tell her about the acci-lent," said Philip. "But if she doesn't, I vote we keep 1uiet and just see what happens."

As it turned out, Mrs. Jelf did not ask them anything. Nhen they reached home it was to find that their father 1ad arrived just before them, having got back from the 2ity much earlier than usual. He was far too busy talk-ng about himself to allow anyone else a word in edge-vays. He was like that sometimes, especially when things 1adn't been going well.

"It wasn't the least good trying to get any work done o-day," he complained to Mrs. Jelf as he drank his tea. 'I simply couldn't concentrate on anything."

Mrs. Jelf made sympathetic noises.

"You didn't hear anything from Sir Sigismund, I sup-•ose?" she said. "I thought he might perhaps have——"

"Sir Sigismund!" said Mr. Jelf so violently that he pilled some of his hot tea on his trousers, which did not mprove his temper. "I should think I have heard from iim! That's the whole of the trouble. There was a letter at the office by the midday post—he must have written it as soon as he got home last night—to say that on careful consideration he had decided that the proposition I had put before him did not appeal to him. I don't believe it for a moment. For one thing, he hadn't had the time to consider an important project like that carefully. It was simply that he'd lost his temper over Philip's piece of stupidity last night. He was quite different when I was talking to him."

"Don't you think if you could talk to him again you might make things all right?" Mrs. Jelf said.

This well-meant suggestion only made Mr. Jelf angrier than ever. "I rang the fellow up at his office as soon as I got his letter," he said, "and I was told he was too busy to see me. I tried again after lunch and they said he had gone down to the country. I'm sure he is trying to avoid me. If I could only see him, just for five minutes . . ."

Mr. Jelf went on talking in this strain for a great deal more than five minutes, and it made Philip and Mary feel worse every time he repeated it. "If he could only see Sir Sigismund," indeed! If only they could! Finally by way of a diversion, Philip said, "Do you mind if we put on the wireless, Daddy? It's just time for the six o'clock news."

"I suppose you can if you want to," said his father moodily.

They listened to the news without any great interest until at the end the announcer said: "Here is a police message. Missing from his home at Great Mattress Slumbershire, Sir Sigismund Kaufman-Fortescue, the well-known financier. Aged sixty-two, five feet four inches high, heavily built and bald. He was last seen wearing a checked tweed suit with a pink carnation in the button-hole. Sir Sigismund was due this afternoon to address a meeting at the Memorial Hall, Eiderdown. He attended the meeting, but shortly after commencing his speech he left the platform somewhat suddenly, and has not since been seen. He is believed to be suffering from loss of memory. Will any person having news of his whereabouts please communicate with the Chief Constable of Slumber-shire, telephone number Bedstead 6666, or with the nearest police station."

"That," said Mr. Jelf savagely, as he turned off the wireless, "that puts the lid on it!"

CHAPTER TEN

AT THE POLICE-STATION

★

Mary slept in a little room of her own at the top of the house. It had two windows, a large one that looked out on to the garden and a small one that faced in the direction of the village. There was a high hedge which cut off the view of the road, but at one place there was a gap in it where a tree had blown down the winter before, so that the head of anyone passing along was just visible at that point from the small window. Consequently this window was Mary's favourite. Standing on tiptoe, with her chin on a level with the window-sill, she could pick out the postman's flat cap as he trudged up with the morning's letters, or the tousled yellow hair of the boy who delivered the newspaper, or the head and shoulders of the milkman, standing up in his cart as he went his round. Often after breakfast she would run up to her room to catch a glimpse of her father's black felt hat bobbing up and down as he scampered down the road to the bus stop on his way to work. It gave her a deliciously superior feeling to be able to peep out at all those people without their knowing that they were being observed, all the more so because she had found by experiment that this was the only window in the house from which this particular view was to be had. What was more, she had never told anybody else about it, not even Philip, who was sometimes mystified by the way in which she always seemed to know to a minute when the post was going to come—especially at Christmas, when the post is exceptionally important.

On the morning after their memorable visit to Eiderdown, Mary was finishing dressing and at the same time engaged in her favourite occupation of spying on the road from the village. This naturally made dressing a rather slow and chancy business, since it is extremely difficult to look at two things at once, and buttons that are done up by feel have a habit of connecting with the wrong buttonholes. But without knowing why, Mary felt certain that it was especially important that morning to keep her eyes on the gap in the hedge, even if it meant making her late for breakfast. She had no idea who she was likely to see, whether it would be their car-driver coming back full of apologies to return the bottle, or Sir Sigismund himself, just released from captivity, on his way to explain to Mr. Foliot-Foljambe why he had left his meeting so suddenly, or—worst of all—the sinister brown-faced stall-keeper still in search of the "vairy fonny bottle" that he had tried to steal, but she was sure there would be someone.

She was trying to kick her feet into her shoes without looking down when a head appeared in the gap. It belonged to none of the people she had thought of, but all the same her heart gave a jump. For the head was that of a policeman, and he was coming up the road towards the house. There was no mistaking the shape of his helmet. Mary thought very hard for a moment, and then, without waiting even to do up her shoes, she ran quickly downstairs. In the hall she stopped and listened for a moment. There was a frizzly sound of frying from the kitchen, which meant that her mother was cooking breakfast, as Mrs. Marrable was still on her holiday. From the bathroom came the sound of her father stropping his razor. She could hear Philip banging about in his bedroom. The coast was clear. Without further hesitation Mary flew out of the front door, out of the garden gate and into the road. She met the policeman just before he reached the house.

The policeman eyed her rather strangely. "Hullo!" he said. "You're out rather early, aren't you, miss?"

"Please," said Mary, "were you coming to see me?"

The policeman looked at her again, and this time there was a twinkle in his eye. He pulled a piece of paper out of his pocket, consulted it, and then said, "Miss Mary Jelf?"

"Yes. That's me."

"Master Philip Jelf?"

"That's my brother. He's still indoors."

The policeman folded the paper up and put it away.

"I've been sent up to ask your father and mother——" he began.

"Oh, please don't!" Mary said quickly.

"There's nothing for you to be frightened of," said the policeman kindly. "It's simply to ask them if they'd arrange for you two to step down to the station for a minute or two—after you've had your breakfast and perhaps tidied up a bit," he added, with another amused glance at Mary.

"But you needn't ask *them*," said Mary earnestly. "It's *us* you want, isn't it? And of course we'll come."

"Ah," said the policeman, "that's all very well, but we can't go fetching boys and girls down to police stations without telling their fathers and mothers, can we? Some people wouldn't like it, and I'm sure your father and mother wouldn't." And he started to move in the direction of the house.

"If you did tell them they'd simply hate it!" said Mary.

Her voice must have sounded pretty desperate, for the policeman stopped and looked at her.

"Eh?" he said.

"Look here," Mary went on. "Is what you want to see me and Philip about something to do with what happened to Mr. Chaffers yesterday?"

"Well," said the policeman, "suppose it is. I tell you, missy, there's nothing at all for you to be frightened about——"

"I'm *not* frightened," Mary protested. "And no more is Philip. And I do promise we'll tell you everything—everything you want to know, that is. It's simply that—well, it'll make everything so complicated if Daddy and Mummy are brought into it." One of her shoes was coming off and she hopped up and down trying to shuffle back into it. "Daddy's *very* worried just now and it's most important that he shouldn't be upset or anything," she added in her most appealing voice.

The policeman was looking quite sympathetic by now, but he was still doubtful.

97

"That's all very well," he said, "and I'm sure we don't want to upset anybody, but we have to keep to rules, you know. There's a rule that juveniles are not to be interviewed except in the presence of a parent or guardian. Our inspector is very strict about it."

Mary suddenly had an idea.

"Parent or guardian?" she said. "Is that a regulation?"

"That's right, miss."

"Solidified?"

"I beg your pardon, miss?"

"Never mind. The point is, a guardian is as good as a parent?"

"Nothing's as good as a parent," said the policeman solemnly. "Nothing in the world."

"I mean, when it comes to interviewing ju—ju——"

"Juveniles, is the word, miss."

"Juveniles, then—a guardian counts as a parent in the regulation?"

"That's so."

"All right, then. Mr. Chaffers will be the guardian. He'll have to be at the interview, because he was the person who had the accident, and he can guard me and Philip beautifully and Daddy and Mummy needn't know anything about it!"

The policeman said nothing for a moment. His face had gone rather red and his shoulders were shaking. He took off his helmet and wiped his forehead with his handkerchief. Then he said, "You win, missy. I don't know what the inspector will say if this comes to his ears, but I'll take the risk. Will you promise that you and your brother will be down at the station at ten o'clock sharp?"

"I swear we will," said Mary. "Honest Afreet."

"Eh?"

"Nothing, it's just a private swear-word," Mary explained.

This time the policeman laughed out loud, but he seemed satisfied, and Mary ran back to the house as fast as she could.

"You're late for breakfast again, Mary," Mr. Jelf complained as she entered the dining-room. "Why can't you get up in good time?"

Considering that she had got up specially early and had done what felt like a good day's work already, Mary considered that this was decidedly unfair, but she made no reply. In any case, her father was far too busy eating his breakfast in double quick time so as not to miss his bus to expect any answer. Her mother was different. She took one quick look at Mary and said,

"Good gracious, Mary, what has come over you? Your frock's buttoned up crooked, you haven't combed your hair properly and—really! at your age!—you've actually got your shoes on the wrong feet!" (So *that's* why my feet felt so uncomfortable while I was talking to the policeman, thought Mary.) "One would think you had never been taught how to dress yourself," her mother went on. "Go upstairs, and please don't come down again until you are respectable!"

Mary obediently went up to her room, and when she looked in the glass she had to admit that her mother was justified, and she began to understand why the policeman had stared at her so strangely. It is extraordinary what a difference it makes to dressing when you are looking out of the window all the time instead of at yourself.

By the time she had put things to rights, her father had left the house. As soon as possible after breakfast she told Philip her news. He was pleased and excited.

"If they want us down at the police station," he said, "it must be because they've caught the man who knocked Mr. Chaffers over, and that means they've found his car and *that* means they've found the bottle, too. So everything's just perfect! Thank goodness you managed to head the policeman off seeing Daddy and Mummy! Now we shall be able to put everything right without their knowing anything about it."

"We can't be sure yet about getting Sir Sigismund back," said Mary cautiously. "After all, the man may have opened the bottle. You said it would be the first thing he would do, didn't you?"

"Well, I was jolly well wrong, then," declared Philip. "Because if he'd opened it he'd have had a wish, and if he'd had a wish, the first thing he'd have wished for would have been that the police shouldn't catch him, and they have."

This reasoning quite convinced Mary, and it was with high hopes that the two of them made their way to the village. At the police-station they found the sergeant whom they had seen the day before and the policeman who had met Mary that morning. They were talking together and appeared to be enjoying a private joke.

"I'm afraid you'll have to wait a little," the sergeant told them. "Your guardian isn't here yet."

Presently Mr. Chaffers arrived. He had a piece of sticking-plaster on his forehead and he was still limping, but he was quite cheerful.

"Ah!" he exclaimed. "So you've got the ruffian, have you? That's a smart piece of work, sergeant, a very smart piece of work!"

"Well," said the sergeant modestly, "it wasn't such a very difficult job, really. Was it?" he added, turning to the other policeman.

"Lord bless you, no, sergeant!" said the policeman with a laugh.

"How did you catch him?" asked Mr. Chaffers eagerly. "Did he show fight?"

"You tell him, constable," said the sergeant.

Mary's policeman drew himself up very stiffly, looked fixedly at the opposite wall, put his hands to his sides, and began to recite in a strange sing-song voice:

"At five forty-two p.m. on Wednesday the ninth instant in consequence of a telephone message received from the omnibus terminus at Bedstead I proceeded by bicycle to a point on the main Little Bolster–Bedstead road approximately one and a quarter miles to the north-east of Little Bolster and one hundred yards south-west of the Pillow cross-roads omnibus stop arriving there at six five p.m."

He stopped to take breath and then went on as before.

"The road at this point describes a sharp right-hand turn and I observed that the hedge on the left-hand side of the road had been broken down indicating that a large object had recently passed through it. Dismounting from my bicycle I proceeded through the hedge where I found

ten-horse-power saloon motor-car index number A.D.
en sixty-six stationary in a ploughed field. In the driver's
eat of the motor-car I found the prisoner. He was asleep
ınd I formed the opinion that he was under the influence
ɔf alcohol."

"What did I tell you?" exclaimed Mr. Chaffers. The
ɔoliceman frowned at him, and then looked back at the
ᴠall and went on:

"I awakened him and he gave his name as William
Catchpole National Registration number ABCK Six
Eight One aged thirty-five chicken farmer residing at the
Henneries Sleepy Hollow Bedstead. I procured assistance
ınd conveyed him to the police station. He was there

charged with being drunk in charge of a motor vehicle driving to the danger of the public failing to stop after an accident and wilful damage to a hedgerow growing upon the verge of a public highway. He was cautioned and said"—here the policeman produced a note-book thumbed over the leaves until he found the place he wanted, and then read—" 'Yes' ". He put the note-book back in his pocket and concluded, "The car which was in a damaged condition was subsequently conveyed to the police station."

The policeman unstiffened himself, to show that the recitation was over.

"Ah!" said Mr. Chaffers.

"But what really happened?" asked Mary, who was quite bewildered by all the long words.

"I've just told you, 'aven't I?" said the constable in quite a human voice. "This chap Catchpole, when he got outside the village, went sound asleep in his car and drove through the 'edge at the corner. The bus driver saw the car in the field with him inside it and tipped us off when he got to the end of his run. So I went off and brought him in. That's all."

"It sounds much easier that way," remarked Philip.

"It doesn't do to make things sound too easy," said the sergeant reprovingly. "Our inspector doesn't like it. And now," he went on in an official voice, "bring in William Catchpole!"

The policeman darted out through a door in the back and came back in a moment with a man whom the children at once recognized as their driver of the day before. He looked a sorry figure. His clothes were stained and crumpled, his face was quite pale and he had a very sheepish expression.

" 'Ullo kids," said William Catchpole in a rather hoarse voice. "Sorry about yesterday. 'Ope you got 'ome all right." He looked at Mr. Chaffers, and seemed more sheepish than ever. "No bones broke, I 'ope, chum?" he said. "All my fault, I own. I 'ad a drop too much in the Market."

At a nod from the sergeant, the constable took him away again.

"So that's that!" said the sergeant in a satisfied tone. "There'll be no more trouble now. You can run along home, kids. Thank you for coming down."

The children didn't in the least want to run along home yet.

"Please," said Philip, "can we have a look at the car? We left something of ours in it, and it's frightfully important."

The sergeant led them to a yard at the back of the police station. Mr. Chaffers came with them. There was the car, looking shabbier than ever. Its radiator was smashed in, there were scratches and dents all along its sides, and where its headlamps ought to have been were some tangled bits of the hedge. The sergeant opened the back and the children saw the familiar jumble of odd-ments which they remembered from the day before. Everything had been thrown on the floor in confusion. Philip reached inside and pulled out the smelly horse rug and then the sack of chicken food, which were on top of the heap. That left still a lot of other things. He found first a dog-collar with brass studs on it, next a pony's halter, then a wireless battery, a tin of kerosene (which had leaked), a stone hot-water bottle, a newspaper parcel smelling strongly of fish, a packet of breakfast cereal, a bag of very squashy tomatoes and a new garden trowel. There was nothing else. Absolutely nothing. He turned to Mary with a very white face.

"It's gone," he said. "The bottle isn't there any more."

CHAPTER ELEVEN

FOOT-PRINTS IN THE PLOUGH

★

"It's gone," Philip repeated, looking utterly woebegone.

"Ah!" rumbled Mr. Chaffers sympathetically.

Mary said nothing, because she was sure that if she opened her mouth she would start to howl, and she was determined not to break down in front of the police sergeant.

"Well," said Philip at last, "I suppose we'd better be getting home now."

They trailed dismally out of the police station yard.

Mr. Chaffers followed them. He was obviously sorry for their disappointment and did his best to comfort them.

"I'll look about at Bolster Place this afternoon," he said. "Maybe there's another of them bottles lying about."

"No," said Philip wretchedly, "I'm quite sure there isn't. But thank you, all the same," he added.

"You're quite sure it was in the car?" Mr. Chaffers asked.

"Oh yes, it was in the car all right. And while that Catchpole person was asleep someone must have pinched it."

"Ah?" said Mr. Chaffers, in a rather unbelieving tone, "and what should make anyone want to steal a thing like that, I wonder?"

"Well, you see," Philip said, "this was rather a special sort of bottle."

"It was frightfully valuable," put in Mary, who had decided to take Mr. Chaffers at least partly into their confidence. "A man in the market at Eiderdown wanted to give us twenty pounds for it."

"Ah!" There was no doubt that Mr. Chaffers was now thoroughly impressed with the seriousness of the matter.

"And what's more," Mary went on, "I bet that he's the man who's pinched it!"

"The ruffian!" said Mr. Chaffers. "How do you make that out?"

But Mary, full of her idea, was by now talking to Philip rather than to him.

"Don't you see?" she said. "He must have seen us going off in Catchpole's car and followed along by the next bus."

"But," said Philip, "he saw us when we were walking through the village. If he was after us, he'd have got off at the Seven Sleepers."

"He wasn't after us. He was after the bottle, and he could see we hadn't got it with us then. He went on——"

"By Jove, yes!" Philip interrupted. "Didn't your policeman say the car was just this side of the Pillow cross-roads stop? If he got out there, he'd have seen the car for certain. Ten to one he went back to have a look and that's when he pinched the bottle. Oh, Lord, Mary! This is awful! If he's got it, we shall never see it again!"

Mr. Chaffers, meanwhile, had been turning his head from side to side, listening first to one child and then to the other, with growing perplexity.

"Here," he said. "Who is this fellow, anyway?"

"A man in the Market," Philip explained. "He had a stall of china and glass and things. He was brown and eastern-looking and talked in a queer, foreign way."

"Ah!" said Mr. Chaffers. "I know the sort. Real flibbertigibbets, they are. I've seen 'em about the markets hereabouts. Here to-day and gone to-morrow. But if you want to catch him, why don't you tell this smart policeman fellow? Maybe he could lay his hands on him."

Philip shook his head. "No," he said. "It's no good telling the police about this. Even if they did find him, it wouldn't be any good. It's the bottle we want, and if we don't get hold of that soon, it'll be too late, anyway."

"Well," said Mr. Chaffers, looking more puzzled than ever, "you know your business best, I suppose. But if I ever lay my hands on this fellow, I'll——Hold on, though!" he added. "We don't know for sure that this thing is stolen, do we? Suppose it had just been thrown out of the car when it went through the hedge? It may be there still."

"Oh, Philip, do you think it might?" cried Mary.

"There's always a chance," said Philip. "We ought to have thought of that before."

"I'll just run over there this afternoon on my bicycle and have a look," said Mr. Chaffers. "No, dash it! I'd forgot. Of course, I can't now, along of that Catchpole feller, and it's too far for me to walk with this leg of mine. I tell you what, though, I've just remembered, I've a couple of men going over Pillow way to do a little job of painting. They can give us a lift out in the van and wait

while we have a look round. You can walk home and I'l
go on to Pillow to see how the job's going there."

"If you're sure that's not too much trouble," said
Philip, but Mr. Chaffers shook his head.

"If that bottle's worth twenty pounds, it's worth a little
trouble," he said. "And I shan't forget in a hurry how
you helped me when I had that tumble yesterday."

At that they parted, agreeing to meet at Mr. Chaffers's
builder's yard at two o'clock that afternoon.

When they arrived at the yard, the children found a
van drawn up, already almost entirely filled with ladders
planks, pots of paint and two agreeable young men called
Bert and Curly. Bert had bright red hair, and Curly, in
spite of being young, was quite bald. They made room
for the children on two benches which ran the length of
the van, while Mr. Chaffers sat in front with the driver
The inside of the van, which was covered in over the top
and open at the back, was rather stuffy, but smelled
deliciously of paint and turpentine. On the way, Bert
read a paper called *The Greyhound Racing Special*, and
Curly sang very melodiously a song of which the first
words were, "If you'll be my honey, I'll be your bread
and butter man," but as he always broke down after a
few bars and had to start again, Philip and Mary never
learned any more of it, much as they would have liked to

Presently the van stopped and Mr. Chaffers came round
to the back. The children got out and the van drove away
round the corner.

"I told him it was dangerous to stop on the bend,"
explained Mr. Chaffers. "So it is, but I wasn't going to

have those young fellers laughing at me, going treasure-hunting at my time of life."

There was no doubt that they were at the right place. Right in the middle of the corner there was a huge gaping hole in the hedge, just as the policeman had said, and leading up to and away from it were the tyre-marks of a car, some of them surrounded by lumps of squashed mud, which showed where the car had gone when the police came to tow it out of the ploughed field.

Philip and Mary followed Mr. Chaffers through the gap and into the field on the other side. Here the tyre marks became much deeper, and there was a big depression where the car had sunk down into the soft ground and flattened the ridges of earth. On every side were the large foot-prints of the men who had hauled the car away.

They looked everywhere—on the side of the road, in the ditch, in the hedge and in the furrows of the plough itself. But nowhere did they find anything, except some broken bits of glass, which had evidently come from the lamps or windscreen of the unlucky car.

"You're sure you did leave it in the car?" Mr. Chaffers asked again, when it was clear that their search was fruitless.

"Yes," said the children in weary unison.

"Then I'm afraid it does look as though someone's gone off with it," said Mr. Chaffers. "You can go on looking if you like, but I must be getting on, or Bert and Curly will be wondering what's become of me." He was turning to go, when he stopped. "Just a minute," he said. "What do you make of that?"

He was pointing to the ground at a spot a little further inside the field than where the car had lain. It was a rather blurred mark on the top of a ridge of plough, and it certainly looked like a light foot-print.

"No policeman ever made that," said Mr. Chaffers. He squatted down and looked along the ground, shading his eyes from the sun. "Look!" he said.

Philip and Mary squatted down, too, and followed with their eyes the direction in which he was pointing. Then they could see, running across the field, a line of similar little marks, just denting the top of each ridge.

"Someone's walked along that way," said Philip.

"Ah!" said Mr. Chaffers. "But which way?"

They followed the track a short distance, and it was not long before they found the undoubted mark of a slender toe. Whoever left the foot-prints had evidently been walking away from the car.

"Follow along and see where it leads to," said Mr. Chaffers. "It's no good asking me to walk on this plough-land."

Philip ran off across the field. Once he had picked it up, it was easy to follow the track. Mary was soon out-distanced and returned to Mr. Chaffers. Presently they saw Philip coming back.

"The track went through the hedge at the end of the field," he said as soon as he came up with them. "There's a hard lane on the other side, and I couldn't follow it beyond that. But I've found something—look!"

He held up a small, bright object.

"Oh, but I've seen that before!" said Mary at once.

"It's—it's—I know, it's the tie-pin that man at the stall was wearing!"

"He must have dropped it getting through the hedge,"

said Philip. "There's no doubt now who's got the bottle, Mary."

"No," said Mary forlornly, "there isn't. Oh, Philip, how rotten it all is!"

"It's a pretty pin, anyway," Mr. Chaffers pointed out, in a well-meant attempt to cheer them up. "And I reckon you're entitled to keep it. Well, I don't pay Bert and

Curly two and sevenpence an hour with overtime at a time and a half to hang about in the van while I go trapesing over fields and hedges. I must be off."

The children shook hands with him on the road.

"Perhaps I'll be seeing you again at Bolster Place soon," he said. "You know your Granny's moving in next week? Ah! You won't know the place when we've finished tidying it up."

Then he limped round the corner to where Curly was still trying to get the tune of "If you'll be my honey, I'll be your bread and butter man," and they heard the van drive away.

"Well," said Philip, as they faced the walk home, "we've got a tie-pin to show for it, anyhow. We'll have to take turns to wear it, Mary. But it isn't much compared with the bottle. Ten thousand pounds! Poor Daddy!"

"And poor Sir Sigismund!" sighed Mary.

CHAPTER TWELVE

AN OLD FRIEND REAPPEARS

*

"D o you realize, Mary," said Philip, "that we've got to go back to school the day after to-morrow?"

"Of course I do," said Mary. She had indeed been thinking of little else for the last three days. It was on Thursday that they had made the fatal discovery in the ploughed field. This was Monday, and their holidays came to an end on Wednesday. Friday, Saturday and Sunday had been awful. The papers had been full of the disappearance of Sir Sigismund, especially the Sunday ones, which had the most blood-curdling suggestions about his possible fate. The police were hunting for him everywhere, rivers had been dragged, bloodhounds had sniffed vainly all round Great Mattress and the Memorial Hall at Eiderdown and the wireless had repeated the message about him so often they that all knew it by heart. It was dreadful to the children to have so much vital knowledge bottled up inside them and not be able to do anything about it. It was still worse to see their father getting every day more and more worried and anxious and to know that they were really responsible for his trouble. The fact that he never dreamed of connecting them with Sir Sigismund vanishing only made them feel more wretched. Indeed, if it hadn't been for the possibility that they might still be able to put things right, they

would have been only too glad to get away from home
and go back to their respective schools that very day.

"The day after to-morrow," Philip repeated. "That
only leaves us one day to do anything in."

"Two days," Mary corrected him.

"No, only one. To-day we're going to London for the
dentist and the theatre."

"Of course," said Mary, "I'd forgotten."

It showed how upsetting the last few days had been
that Mary should have forgotten that. The dentist was
nothing—he was a particularly nice man and hardly ever
hurt at all—but the theatre was by long-standing custom
the final fling of the summer holidays. In the ordinary

way, Philip and Mary looked forward to it with tremendous excitement. But now it simply meant one more precious chance missed of doing something towards straightening out the tangle in which they found themselves, and they almost wished they were not going.

There is, however, something about a theatre that just can't fail to cheer you up, however gloomy you may have been beforehand. Mrs. Jelf had been quite worried about the children's lack of enthusiasm on the way up to London, and she had wondered whether they were not both secretly suffering from toothache and afraid that the dentist would have to do something drastic and painful to cure it. But the dentist quickly reassured her on that point, and although they ate a poor lunch for the occasion, once they were in their seats at the theatre, among the lights and bustle and chatter, fingering their programmes and listening to the exciting noise of the orchestra tuning up, they began to look pleased and happy once more.

Then the curtain went up and the children forgot all their troubles at once. It was a gorgeous show, with lots of music and dancing, but not too much of either to get in the way of the most gloriously comic funny man they had ever seen. They rolled about in their seats in laughter and at the end of the first act they were contented, excited—and hot.

"Mummy," said Philip, standing up and twisting round in his place, "there are ices. Shall I see if I can get some?"

"Not for me, thank you," said Mrs. Jelf, fanning herself vigorously with her programme. "But you and Mary can have some if you like."

There were attendants handing ices on trays round the seats, but it was a slow business, and it certainly didn't look as though there would be enough trays to go round. So the children made their way to the back of the theatre from where the ices seemed to be coming, to see if they would have better luck there. At first they thought they were going to be disappointed. The ices were certainly there, but there were so many people clamouring for them that it was impossible to get served. They were hanging rather helplessly round the outskirts of the crowd when they heard a voice behind them that sounded familiar.

"Hullo, you two!" it said. "Are you looking for ices?"

They turned round, and saw a short, pleasant-faced man in a dark suit smiling at them. For a moment or two they did not recognize him, and then memory came back with a rush.

"Djinn, darling!" cried Mary, running across to where he was standing. "It's you!"

"Sh!" said the Djinn quickly. "That is not my name here. Did you say ices?"

"Yes, *please!*" said Mary.

The Djinn, without moving, just lifted his hand and snapped his fingers. Immediately a very pretty attendant pushed her way through the crowd, carrying a tray with two gigantic ices. It was like magic, the children afterwards agreed, and certainly the most satisfying piece of magic they had yet seen.

"Well," said the Djinn, when the ices had disappeared, "and how have things been going since we last met?"

His question brought them back from the enchanted world of the theatre to the troubles and worries that they had left outside.

"Rottenly," said Philip. "Everything's turned out just as badly as it possibly could."

The Djinn looked grave.

"I'm sorry about that," he said. "Tell me."

And then the children realized, with a delicious feeling of relief, that they had found the one person in the world to whom they could explain exactly what had happened without being laughed at or disbelieved. They poured out the whole history of the last week and the Djinn listened to them with serious attention. He did not interrupt or ask any questions, but when they told him of how Sir Sigismund had been wished into the bottle, he threw back his head and laughed out loud.

"Poor old Siggy!" he said. "So that's where he's been all this time! How sick he will be, cooped up in there, thinking of all the chances he's missing of making money!"

His cheerfulness encouraged the children greatly, but they noticed that when they went on to describe the dark-skinned stallkeeper, he frowned and looked very grave again. When they had finished, he said, "Well, I'm truly sorry things have turned out so badly. Wishes are tricky things, you know, and you can never be quite sure how they will work. Still, I don't think the outlook is quite so bad as you imagine. In fact, there's no reason why everything shouldn't come right in the end."

Just then the bell began to ring for the audience to go back to their seats.

"Come and have another chat at the next interval," said the Djinn. "I may be able to tell you a little more when I've thought this over."

The second act was quite as good as the first. Indeed, the children thought it was even better, though this may have been only because meeting the Djinn had put them in such a much happier frame of mind. He seemed to take everything in such a sensible, matter-of-fact way that though he had not promised that he could do anything to help them, they both felt that the situation could not be nearly so desperate as it had seemed during the last three days. It occurred to Philip, while his attention wandered from the stage during a rather long song about love (in which he was not much interested), that by rights they ought to be very cross with the Djinn, as all the trouble was really due to the tiresome wishes he had given them. But, somehow, it was quite impossible to feel cross with him. Not after those ices, anyhow.

When the curtain went down at the end of the second act, Philip and Mary left their seats at once and went to the back. They found the Djinn in the same place, and this time he whistled up two glasses of lemonade before they had even had time to think of it. Then he said:

"There's one very important thing about this business which you don't seem to have realized. It's just four days since the bottle was stolen, and Sir Sigismund is still inside it."

Philip choked over his lemonade. This was a new idea.

"Is he?" he asked. "Are you sure?"

"Obviously. Otherwise he would have reappeared by

now, and be back at his office, hard at work making more money."

"But," said Mary, "we were certain that the man would let him out at once, so as to earn a wish from him."

"That's what you'd expect him to do," agreed the Djinn. "And there can only be one reason why he hasn't done it—and that's because he *can't*."

"Why not?" both children asked at once.

The Djinn smiled and turned to Philip.

"When you corked Siggy up," he asked, "did you say anything, by any chance?"

Philip thought for a moment.

"Yes," he said finally. "I remember now. There wasn't any seal or anything to keep the cork in place, like there was when we found it the first time, so I just jammed it in as hard as I could, and while I was doing it I did say, 'Don't you come out till I tell you to'. It didn't mean anything in particular, it was just for luck."

"It was certainly very lucky for you that you did say it, whether it meant anything or not," the Djinn observed. "You see, being a magic cork—naturally it has to be—it pays attention to what is said to it, and it would take a very competent magician indeed to shift it now without your permission."

"Then what does he want to keep the bottle for if he can't open it?" asked Philip.

The Djinn frowned and shook his head.

"Unfortunately," he said, "there's quite a lot you can do with a Djinn in a bottle, even if you can't get him out. That is, if you know a few simple spells, and are an evilly-disposed person. Now I'm inclined to think that this stall-keeper of yours is a very evilly-disposed person indeed. In fact, I shouldn't be surprised if he belonged to the Aladdin family. You may have heard of it."

"But of course I've heard of Aladdin!" said Mary. "He wasn't at all an evil person. He was very nice."

The Djinn looked very severe.

"Nice?" he said. "Because he married a princess and lived in a palace happily ever after? Is that what they teach you in your history-books? Let me tell you, Aladdin was one of the greatest tyrants and slave-drivers we Djinns have ever known. Just think of his career! Nothing but rubbing his wretched lamp day in and day out and sending his poor Djinn here, there and everywhere on the most impossible errands with never a word of thanks! It was a scandal. Of course things are different now. We Afreets have got decent conditions of labour with proper working hours and paid holidays, but there are still plenty of bad employers left, and believe me, the Aladdins are the worst of them!"

The Djinn had got quite excited in his attack on Aladdin, and seemed for the moment to have forgotten all about Sir Sigismund, until Mary reminded him by saying, "You don't think he'll *hurt* Sir Sigismund, do you?"

"No," replied the Djinn, calming down at once. "He won't be able to hurt him physically, because you can't hurt a ball of smoke, especially when it's protected by a burglar-proof bottle. But I expect he'll be hurting his feelings pretty badly, making him do all kinds of low jobs for him, like conjuring and fortune-telling, which must be most wounding to a Djinn who's a millionaire and a B.A. at that."

"Is there anything you can do to help?" asked Philip hopefully.

The Djinn shook his head.

"No," he said. "We're not allowed to interfere with the working out of wishes. That's one of the strictest regulations. But don't worry. Everything will sort itself out in time, and perhaps it will not be such a long time as you think."

That was all he could tell them, for by now the third and last act was due to begin and the children only just got back to their seats in time, after the lights had been turned down and trampling on several people's toes in the process.

On the whole, they enjoyed the third act more than either of the others. The funny man was more amusing than ever, and, best of all, he sang the whole of the words and music of "If you'll be my honey, I'll be your bread and butter man." Philip was determined to learn it by heart so that he could teach Curly next time they met, and he hummed it all the way down in the train. But, like Curly, he always forgot how it went after the first few bars. It was that sort of tune.

When they reached home, their father was already back from the City. They found him reading the evening paper with a gloomy expression. He hardly paid any attention when the children tried to tell him about the theatre, and he only came out from behind his newspaper when Mrs. Jelf, going through the letters, exclaimed, "Here's an invitation from Mother!"

"What's the Unpredictable up to now?" he asked,

quite forgetting that Philip and Mary were not supposed
to know that that was her nickname.

Mrs. Jelf pursed her lips and frowned at his lapse, and
then said, "She wants us all to come over to tea at Bolster
Place to-morrow."

"Come over to tea? What nonsense! She hasn't even
moved in yet," said Mr. Jelf.

"The letter says that she is moving her furniture
to-day," Mrs. Jelf explained. "It's written on a packing-
case, apparently, and to judge from the hand-writing
I should say it had been written in a furniture van,
too."

"Surely the place won't be fit for a tea-party by to-
morrow," said Mr. Jelf. "What's the hurry?"

"I was just coming to that," Mrs. Jelf went on
patiently. "It's the Little Bolster and Featherbed
Women's Institute annual fête——"

"What the deuce!" interrupted Mr. Jelf, who had
quite forgotten his paper by now.

"Mother had quite forgotten that she had offered to
lend them the garden for it, but apparently it has all been
arranged for some time and she can't get out of it now.
There's to be a Punch and Judy show and a fortune-
teller and a houp-la——"

"—and a baby-show and morris dancing and an address from the vicar," suggested Mr. Jelf.

"She doesn't mention them, but I should think it's
quite likely. Anyhow, the point is, we are all to go, and
when we have had enough of it, we are to come in to tea
and be shown all over the house. You would like to go,
wouldn't you, children?"

"Rather!" said Philip. It sounded quite an amusing way to spend the last day of the holidays.

"And I'm sure you'd like to see the house, George," said Mrs. Jelf to her husband. "You can take half a day off from the office. You said yourself only the other day that there was nothing to do there."

But Mr. Jelf had retired behind his newspaper again.

"I can't possibly do it," he said.

"But why not? It would do you good to take your mind off business for an afternoon."

"I've got an appointment in the afternoon at four o'clock."

Something in his voice made Mrs. Jelf look up.

"George!" she said sharply. "Who is your appointment with?"

"As a matter of fact," Mr. Jelf mumbled unwillingly from behind the paper, "I'm going to see MacSwindle."

"MacSwindle! That horrid man who cheated you so dreadfully when you invented the collapsible butter-dish? You can't really be meaning to go and ask him for money again?"

Both parents had by now quite forgotten that the children were in the room. Philip and Mary listened with all their ears, hoping they would find out what it was all about before they were noticed and sent off to bed.

"Yes, I *am* going to borrow from MacSwindle!" declared Mr. Jelf, throwing the newspaper on the floor and stamping on it. "Of course I know the man will rob me right and left, but where else am I to go for money to float the new invention now that this Kaufman-Fortescue fellow has vanished? And if I don't get the invention going, there'll be no money to pay Mrs. Marrable's wages or the children's school fees or anything else! I tell you, I'm in a desperate situation—desperate!"

It was at that point that Mrs. Jelf looked round and said quietly, "Darlings, I think it's time you went upstairs to bed."

Philip and Mary went at once, feeling rather subdued and frightened by what they had heard. Philip, indeed, looked so depressed that Mary, when she kissed him good night, felt that she must try to cheer him up.

"I'm certain it'll turn out all right," she said. "The Djinn said so, and I'm sure we can trust him."

"Huh!" said Philip. "You only say that because he gave you an ice."

Which was really grossly unfair of him, for he had had an ice, too, and enjoyed it quite as much as she had.

CHAPTER THIRTEEN

THE FÊTE

★

Mrs. Jelf and the children got to Bolster Place about three o'clock the next afternoon. They found Mrs. Thwaites sitting on her shooting-stick in the middle of the lawn, talking to the vicar of Featherbed.

"So here you are!" she said. "I'm glad you brought the children. They'll find plenty to amuse them, I think. I daren't leave the lawn myself, I'm keeping guard over the sundial. The boys will try to use it for leap-frog. They've nearly had it down twice already."

There were indeed a lot of children in the garden, and

some of them were quite rowdy enough to justify Mrs
Thwaites's apprehension. But most of them were gathered
round the Punch and Judy show, which had just started
in another corner of the garden, or the houp-la stall near
by. Their mothers and elder sisters and aunts—the
Women's Institute members whose outing it really was—
were more interested in walking round the garden, looking at Mrs. Worsley-Worsley's flower-beds (which were
going to be much brighter next year, now they were Mrs
Thwaites's) or criticizing one another's work, displayed
on a stall of Women's Institute handicraft. Some of them
made their way by twos and threes to the far end of the
lawn, where there was a little canvas enclosure, with a
notice outside reading "Madame Anna La Dean, Palm-
ist and Crystal Gazer." Altogether, the garden seemed
alive with people wherever one looked, while from the
house came noises of bumping and banging which
showed that furniture shifting and curtain hanging was
still going on there.

Philip and Mary tried their luck at the houp-la, without very much success, and then listened to the Punch
and Judy show for a time. But for some reason they did
not stay very long there either. It is always like that on
the last day of the holidays. There are so many things you
would like to do and so little time to do them in, that in
the end you are apt to fidget the time away and your last
chance of doing anything is gone before you know where
you are. But on this occasion it was even worse than
usual. They both felt that they ought to be doing *something*, only they couldn't tell what. It made them feel
restless and unhappy. Philip found that his head was

beginning to ache a little. It was a very warm afternoon, and when he looked up to the sky he could see some dark clouds beginning to form just over the horizon. Perhaps there was thunder about, he thought. But his feeling of uneasiness was not wholly accounted for by that.

It was Mary who put into words what was at the back of both their minds.

"Philip," she said, as they drifted away from the Punch and Judy, "I can't help thinking about poor Sir Sigismund. If you're the only person who can let him out of the bottle, then perhaps he'll have to stay a prisoner for years and years."

"For ever, perhaps," said Philip gloomily. "I may never find the bottle. Do you think the spell will be broken when I die?"

"But the Djinn did say that things would turn out all right in the end," said Mary.

"Oh, the Djinn said——" retorted Philip, rather scornfully. "Anyhow, what does 'coming right in the end' mean? In a hundred years or so, I shouldn't wonder. These people probably don't count time the same as we do. What may be quite soon to him may be too late for us and much too late to help Daddy. I don't suppose he knows this is the last day of the holidays."

At this moment their grandmother came up to them.

"How are you getting on?" she said. "I've left Mr. Chaffers on sentry-go at the sun-dial, so I'm free to move about a bit. He's been helping me to lay carpets all day. Do you know the Turkey carpet is just too long for the hall, after all? There's a horrid wrinkle in one end. So provoking! Mr. Chaffers is going to see what he can do about it."

The children were not very much interested in the Turkey carpet, though they were too polite to say so. What was really important was that Mr. Chaffers had evidently not said anything about their part in his accident with Catchpole's motor-car, and they were grateful to him for that.

"What would you like to do?" Mrs. Thwaites went on, evidently noticing that the children looked rather bored and worried. "Your mother's over there, if you want to talk to her. Oh, no, better not. She's with Mrs. Foliot-Foljambe, that very stout lady in the feathered hat. I don't recommend her. I tell you what, though—why not go and have your fortunes told by Madame la Dean? I hear she's wonderful. She charges a shilling each. Here's the money," and she fished a florin out of her bag.

"Thanks awfully, Granny, we will," said Philip, though both he and Mary could have thought of better things to do with the money than having their fortunes told. Still, it was something to do, and they walked across the lawn to Madame la Dean's little canvas cubicle.

As they approached it, two Women's Institute members were just coming away. One of them they recognized as the stout woman on the Eiderdown bus. She looked flushed and angry.

"The things that woman told me!" she was saying. "I never heard such impertinence in all my born days. It ought to be put down, that kind of thing, it ought indeed! And then to take money for insulting you to your face!"

"Well, Emma," said her friend, who seemed rather

amused, "I'm sure all the things she told me were true enough. It was wonderful what she could see in that crystal of hers, I thought."

"True!" replied the bus woman. "Why, that's just what I'm complaining of! Who wants to hear the truth about themselves, I'd like to know?"

They moved away, still arguing. Just as the children approached the cubicle, Madame la Dean stuck her head out and said in a guttural voice, "Any more? I can't wait here all day!"

She was an odd-looking creature, with bright red hair and a face so covered with powder that it was impossible to tell what it was like underneath. She wore a pair of rather dirty white gloves, and what could be seen of the rest of her was covered in a flowing dress of oriental stuff.

"Yes, please!" said Mary. "We want our fortunes told."

"One at a time!" retorted Madame la Dean. She pointed a gloved finger at Philip. "You! I will take you first. And you!" pointing at Mary, "you will wait outside."

So to her disappointment Mary had to hang about outside the enclosure while Philip's fortune was being told. But to her pleasure and surprise, Mr. Chaffers came up at that moment, looking much better, though he still had to walk with a stick.

"I thought you were keeping guard on the sun-dial," she said. "Granny said the boys were trying to play leap-frog on it."

"Ah!" said Mr. Chaffers with a wink. "The vicar, he's giving an address from the lawn just by the sun-dial. I reckon that'll keep the boys away better than I could. Look," he went on. "I've hunted everywhere about the place for another bottle like that one you lost, but there wasn't one. But I have found a little something under the floor boards in the kitchen here, which you'd better have for luck. Here it is."

And he handed Mary a shilling with the head of George III on it and the date, 1792. Mr. Chaffers had cleaned it and polished it until now it was as bright and shining as it had been on the day when someone dropped it, very likely when Bolster Place was being built.

"Oh, thank you, dear Mr. Chaffers!" said Mary. "It is sweet of you, and I'm sure it'll bring me luck. Good gracious!" she added, "whatever's happening?"

Philip meanwhile had entered the fortune-teller's cubicle. Inside it was rather dark and stuffy, and there

vas a strong smell of hot canvas and trodden grass.
Madame la Dean sat behind a small table and there was
another chair in front of it for the visitor. At one side of
he table was a little stand, draped down to the ground
vith muslin, and on this was the crystal in which she
gazed to see visions of the future. It did not look like a
crystal at all, for it was nearly black in colour, but from
time to time it gave out a greenish glow. It was nearly
round in shape, except for the top, which was flat. The
bottom part was hidden by the drapery that covered the
stand.

Philip handed over his florin and Madame la Dean,
after fumbling about in her draperies for some time, produced a shilling change. She was muttering something
under her breath as she did so, and all of a sudden it came
over Philip that he did not like Madame la Dean at all.
There was something very nasty about her. He began to
wish he had not come, but it was too late to do anything
about it now, and in any case he was interested to know
what his fortune would be. Perhaps she could tell him
whether he would find Sir Sigismund, he thought.

"Put your handss on the table, palm upwardss,
pleasse," said Madame la Dean.

Philip obeyed, and as he did so he had the odd feeling
that he had heard something like those words before.
Madame la Dean did not immediately look at his hands.
Instead, her eyes travelled upwards until they met Philip's.
He noticed that they were rather strange, yellow eyes.

"What iss that tie-pin you are wearing?" she asked.
"You must take it off. I cannot tell your fortune while
you wear that pin."

Philip put his hand up to his tie, where was the pin which he had picked up the day after the visit to Eiderdown. He took it out, and as he did so Madame la Dean leaned across the table and snatched it from him so quickly that it had gone before he knew what had happened.

"That iss better!" she said with a horrible grin.

Then something seemed to snap inside Philip's head. The strange, uneasy feeling which he had had all the afternoon and particularly since he had been inside the little tent, suddenly vanished and he knew exactly what had happened.

"You're not Madame la Dean at all!" he exclaimed, jumping up from his chair, "I know who you are. You're——"

The fortune-teller had got up, too, and beneath her powder her face looked very frightened. In the heat the powder had begun to run, and Philip could see streaks of brown skin on her cheeks and neck.

"Pleasse!" she gasped. "Pleasse!"

Philip was leaning across the table, trying to get at the tie-pin, which she was holding in her gloved hands. She tried to avoid him in the confined space of the tent. Between them the table suddenly gave a lurch to one side, and the stand with the crystal on it was upset. With a cry, Madame la Dean pounced on the crystal and caught it as it fell. Then Philip saw that it was not a ball at all, but a round object with a long neck which must have gone through a hole in the top of the stand and been concealed by the drapery that covered it. At the sight of it he forgot all about his tie-pin and everything else.

"Give me my bottle!" shouted Philip and made a grab at the fortune-teller. Some of her flowing skirt tore in his hand as she struggled to get free. The next moment he received a fierce blow in the face, and then the whole tent collapsed on them.

Philip struggled under a mass of canvas and clothing. At times he did not know whether he had hold of the sides of the tent or the fortune-teller's dress. But at last he found himself in the open air again. The first thing he saw

was Madame la Dean, just extricated from the ruins of the tent, her red wig askew and showing short black hair beneath, starting to run across the lawn, the precious bottle under her arm. The next thing he saw was Mary and Mr. Chaffers, standing and staring as though they could not believe their eyes.

"Stop him!" gasped Philip. "Mary, it's Aladdin! The bottle!"

"A-a-ah!" roared Mr. Chaffers, suddenly springing to life. With astonishing agility he hurled himself at the flying form of the fortune-teller. The torn dress was floating behind and this he was just able to seize as the pretended Madame la Dean was making off. The material parted with a loud ripping sound, disclosing a pair of corduroy trousers beneath. But Mr. Chaffers's tug at the dress had been so vigorous that it threw the wearer off his balance and he came to the ground with a heavy fall, letting the bottle slip from his hands. Rolling over and over, Aladdin was up again almost at once. Mr. Chaffers tried to grab his leg, but received a kick in the stomach that winded him completely. The next moment, Aladdin had sprinted across the lawn, leaped the hedge and was lost to sight.

"Ah!" growled Mr. Chaffers, when he could recover his breath. "The villain's got away!"

But Mary was dancing up and down in delight. She had seen the bottle fall and pounced upon it like a hawk.

"It doesn't matter, Mr. Chaffers," she cried. "Nothing matters now! We've got Sir Sigismund again, safe and sound!"

CHAPTER FOURTEEN

SIR SIGISMUND UNBOTTLED

*

The whole garden was in an uproar. From every side women and children came running, all talking at once and at the tops of their voices. The Punch and Judy show was deserted in a moment, and the vicar of Featherbed, in the middle of his address, found himself talking to nothing but a border of zinnias and early Michaelmas daisies. One group clustered round what was left of Madame la Dean's tent, and another surrounded poor Mr. Chaffers as he lay on the ground, all asking him questions which he was far too breathless to answer. Noisiest of the lot was the fat woman from the bus, who waved her arms in the direction in which Aladdin had escaped, and repeated over and over to her friend, "There! What did I tell you!"—though she had certainly not told her anything like what had actually happened.

Philip tugged Mary by the arm. "Let's get out of this, quick!" he said.

They slipped out of the crowd and dodged behind the kitchen garden wall.

"Where are we going?" asked Mary.

"Into the house," said Philip. "That's the only safe place. Come on!"

Following the line of the wall, they soon found themselves at the back door of the house. It was open, and they ran inside unobserved. After the noise and heat of the garden, the house was quiet and cool. What sounds there were came from upstairs, where Mr. Chaffers's men were putting the finishing touches to the decorations. Downstairs, everything looked peaceful and orderly, as though Mrs. Thwaites had been living there for months, instead of having only just moved in. It was difficult to realize that this was the house that they had seen all dusty and deserted a week ago. They sneaked past the door of the kitchen, where they could hear their grandmother's cook moving about, and made their way to the dining-room.

"This will do," said Philip. "Give me the bottle, Mary."

Mary handed him the bottle. Philip put it on the floor and took hold of the cork.

"Just a minute, Philip," said Mary. "I've thought of something."

"What is it?" her brother asked, tugging at the top of the cork. "We can't waste time. Someone may come in any minute."

"It's this," said Mary. "Won't Sir Sigismund be frightfully cross when we let him out?"

"I expect he will be, after all that's happened to him since we put him in the bottle."

"Well, we've never settled—how are we going to make him uncross, so that he'll lend Daddy the money?"

"I don't care whether he's cross or uncross," Philip replied. "I know just what to do. Watch!"

He gave another pull at the cork, but still nothing happened. They could hear the voices of people and footsteps on the gravel path outside the window.

"What's happened?" asked Mary.

"I can't get it out," gasped Philip. And then, "Oh, how silly of me! I forgot! Please, cork, will you come out?"

And immediately the cork obediently loosened itself and came away in his hand quite easily.

Once more Mary watched the thick column of smoke pouring from the neck of the bottle in great puffs. She

noticed that Sir Sigismund's smoke was not quite the same as that of their original Djinn. It had a purplish tinge and was a good deal more agitated; but whether this was due to the shaking the bottle had received or to Sir Sigismund's bad temper, she could not say. Then, to her surprise, the smoke stopped ascending, although only a small cloud had formed about five and a half feet from the ground. Looking down, she saw that Philip, kneeling on the floor, had put the cork back again in the bottle.

"Whatever are you doing?" she asked.

139

"Sh!" said Philip in a whisper. "Wait!"

Presently the cloud grew smaller and solider. Two rather large, fleshy ears formed themselves on either edge. Next a pair of horn-rimmed spectacles materialized, joining the ears, a prominent nose pushed out under the arch of the spectacles, and then all of a sudden there was Sir Sigismund's head suspended in space over the bottle, looking considerably astonished and frowning dreadfully.

"Hi, you! Boy!" said the head. "Let me out of this confounded bottle, will you?"

"Just a second, Sir Sigismund," said Philip, looking up, but keeping his hand carefully on the cork. "If I let you out, will you do us a favour?"

The face went nearly as purple as the smoke had been a moment or two before.

"Do you a favour?" it said. "Do you know who I am?"

"Yes, Sir Sigismund. I know who you are, and I want you to lend Daddy ten thousand pounds."

"Ten thousand——!" The head bounced up toward the ceiling about two feet and then came down again looking rather like a toy balloon on the end of a string. "Good heavens, this is blackmail!"

"No, it's not," said Philip indignantly. "It's simply your fault for losing your temper with Daddy because of a pure accident which he couldn't help because I did it anyway, and it's a jolly good invention and you'll get your money back in no time. Daddy said so."

Sir Sigismund's face looked rather less angry, but very bewildered.

"Accident? Invention?" said the head. "Who are you, and what are you talking about?"

"My name's Philip Jelf."

"Oh . . .! So you're the boy who poured hot coffee on my head, are you?"

"It wasn't coffee, it was cocoa. And anyhow it was an accident that might have happened to anyone."

"And you ought to be jolly grateful to us for getting you away from Aladdin," put in Mary. "Unless you *like* being made to do conjuring tricks and tell people's fortunes."

The head fairly quivered at the mention of Aladdin.

"No, no, my dear children," it said, in an almost humble voice. "I emphatically do not like anything of the kind. Please let me out at once, and in return you shall have a magic wish. Honest Afreet, you shall."

"I'm not fearfully keen on wishes," said Philip. "No more is Mary, after what we've had of them. We'd much rather you lent Daddy ten thousand pounds."

"Ten thousand pounds is a lot of money," said the head doubtfully. "I shall have to consider——"

"Well you'd better be quick about it," said Philip. "You don't want anyone to come in here and find you looking like this."

At that moment, in fact, someone did come in. It was Mrs. Thwaites's parlour-maid with a tray of tea things. She stopped in the doorway and stared, with her mouth wide open in astonishment.

"Go away, woman!" roared Sir Sigismund's voice from mid-air. "Can't you see I'm busy?"

With a wild shriek the parlour-maid dropped the tray and fled from the room. They could hear her footsteps clattering down the passage to the back of the house.

"There you are!" said Philip, when all was quiet again. "Next time it may be Granny, and she'll make much more fuss."

"Oh, very well, very well!" said the head in a resigned voice. "I dare say I shall lose my money, and I still maintain it's blackmail, but I suppose I must put up with it. Now will you let me out?"

Philip released the cork, and bits of Sir Sigismund began to form beneath the head.

"Where do you keep your money?" Philip asked, while the smoke poured upwards to join the rest.

"In the bank, of course," answered Sir Sigismund testily. "But my cheque book is in my coat pocket, if that's what you're thinking of."

"Then I expect that's enough," said Philip, clapping in the cork again. "You can have the rest of you when you've written out the cheque."

And sure enough, Sir Sigismund was now complete down to his waist. The coat and waistcoat of the gay suit were there, complete with the carnation in his buttonhole. Only the trousers were missing.

"I can't sign a cheque in mid-air, can I?" complained Sir Sigismund peevishly. "Give me something to write on."

"The table will do," said Philip. He pushed the bottle across the floor, and Sir Sigismund's upper half followed it. It reminded Mary of a ship she had seen during the war with a barrage balloon attached to its deck. When he got to the table, Philip squatted down underneath it, and Sir Sigismund, holding on to the edge with one hand to keep himself steady, fished out his cheque book with the other.

"Never felt so ridiculous in all my life," he grumbled, as he felt for his fountain pen. "What are your father's initials?"

"A. G." said Philip, from under the table.

"He's Adolphus George," Mary explained. "But Mummy always calls him George."

"And the date? I've lost all count of time in that ghastly bottle."

"The fifteenth of September."

"Thanks."

Sir Sigismund began to write, but before he had filled up the cheque, a high-pitched feminine voice was heard from the hall outside.

"It's quite all right, dear Mrs. Thwaites," it said. "I know you are busy just now. I'll just take a little stroll round by myself."

Then the door opened, and a large lady in a feathered hat came into the room. From the look of her it could be seen that she would give much more trouble than the parlour-maid.

"Sir Sigismund!" she said at once. "Good gracious me! We have been so anxious about you! Where ever have you been? And what——?"

It was an awkward moment, but Sir Sigismund was more than equal to the occasion. He simply looked up from his writing and said quite calmly:

"Ah, Mrs. Foliot-Foljambe! Please excuse my getting up, but, as you see, I am rather busy at this moment. Will you please give my kind regards to your husband and tell him how sorry I was to have been called away so abruptly the other day? And—forgive me—but would you mind closing the door behind you? I am rather susceptible to draughts. Good day!"

Mrs. Foliot-Foljambe was so overcome by Sir Sigismund's masterly demeanour that she withdrew at once, murmuring apologies and looking rather puzzled. She would have been still more puzzled if it had occurred to her to look under the table and had seen Philip crouching on the floor where Sir Sigismund's legs should have been, but luckily she never thought of doing so.

Then Sir Sigismund completed the cheque, and immediately Philip, by taking the cork out of the bottle for the last time, completed Sir Sigismund. No sooner were his legs on again than he got up from the table, stretched imself all over, threw back his head and laughed—and laughed—and laughed.

The children were quite astonished at this sudden change in his behaviour. For a moment they wondered whether his confinement in the bottle and his undignified adventures while inside it had affected his mind. But presently Sir Sigismund's laughter died down, his flabby form stopped shaking and it was apparent that he was quite normal and very pleased with himself.

"Excuse me, my dear children," he said at last, wiping his eyes with a large bandana handkerchief. "But this is really too funny for words. And I've only just realized how very much obliged to you I am!"

Philip and Mary looked at each other in surprise. This was the last thing they had expected him to say.

"How sick it will make all the others!" chortled Sir Sigismund. "They'll be as jealous as cats! Why, I might have waited another hundred years for a chance like this!"

"A chance like what?" Mary asked. But Philip suddenly saw what he was driving at.

"Do you mean a chance to pass your test again?" he asked.

Sir Sigismund nodded, a complacent smile on his plump face.

"Oh, I see," said Mary. "You're a sort of double B.A. now."

"Double B.A. indeed!" said Sir Sigismund scornfully. "I'd have you know, young lady, that I am now entitled to put D.D. after my name, and that's about the highest degree anyone can get."

"What's a D.D.?" asked Philip.

"Doubly Decanted, of course. There's not one Afree
in a thousand who's graduated to that rank. And to thin
that I owe it all to you—it's worth ten thousand any da
of the week! Here's your cheque, young man," he wen
on, handing the cheque to Philip. "Remember me t
your father. Oh, and by the way, I'll have that bottle
please."

"But the Djinn—our Djinn—said we could keep it,
said Mary.

"I dare say he did, but I'm not going to have D.D.'
made too cheap. I'll take it with me. It ought to go bac
for salvage, anyway."

Sir Sigismund picked up the bottle, folded it up exactly
as if it was a piece of paper, and put it in the pocket wher
he kept his cheque book. Then, humming a cheerfu
tune, he strode out of the dining-room into the hall, th
children following. They felt as cheerful as he did, anc
now that the money was safe they did not think that th
bottle was worth worrying about.

They were half-way to the front door when the grand
father clock in the corner struck the hour. Philip stoppec
in his tracks.

"Oh Lord, Mary!" he cried in a voice full of anxiety
"It's four o'clock. I'd quite forgotten—we're too late
after all!"

"What's the matter?" asked Sir Sigismund, stopping
in his turn. "Too late for what?"

"Too late to give Daddy the money. He's gone t
borrow it from someone else, and he's there now."

"If he doesn't want my cheque, I might as well hav

it back," said Sir Sigismund quickly, holding out his hand. "Who was he going to borrow it from?"

"I forget the name," said Philip. "I know Daddy was going to see him at four o'clock."

"It was Mac somebody," said Mary.

"Not MacSwindle, by any chance?"

"Yes, that was it," both children said together.

"MacSwindle, eh?" said Sir Sigismund, slowly. He had a very wide-awake, sharp look on his face. "If Mac-Swindle's in this, it means that there's money in this contraption your father's invented, and Master Mac-Swindle's going to get hold of most of it. He's a nasty piece of work, if ever there was one. I'd rather like to put a spoke in his wheel, if I could, quite apart from anything else."

"It's all very well to say that," said Mary desperately, "but what can we do now? He's there and we're here, and it's past four o'clock already."

It was maddening, thought Philip, to be beaten in this way at the last minute, just when everything seemed to be going so well. He stamped impatiently on the floor. His foot caught in the place where the Turkey carpet was folded because it was too long for the hall, and that reminded him of something.

"Granny wished this carpet was a flying one the other day," he said. "If only it was, we could do something!"

"Well," said Sir Sigismund, with a genial smile, "you're entitled to a wish, aren't you? Why shouldn't it be?"

And of course it was.

CHAPTER FIFTEEN

HOW IT ALL ENDED

★

The carpet rose about two feet in the air and remained motionless, flapping its fringes slowly.

"Where to, guv'nor?" it asked in a hoarse voice.

"MacSwindle's office, 5, Crooks' Corner, Bucket Street, E.C.2," said Sir Sigismund. "And look sharp, we're in a hurry."

"O.K.," said the carpet. "Mind your 'eads!" And it charged straight at the front door, which luckily stood open.

They came out into the garden just as the thunderstorm, which had been threatening all afternoon, broke in a downpour of rain. The carpet shot upwards through sheets of descending water, just above the heads of Mrs. Thwaites and the vicar, who were leading a wild rush of people stampeding into the house for shelter. Luckily they were far too busy trying to avoid the storm to see the carpet careering over them. The children and Sir Sigismund were soaked through in a moment, and the wind was so strong that they had to lie flat to avoid being blown off.

"We'll 'ave to get above this," said the carpet, its husky voice almost drowned in a roll of thunder. "Up we go!"

Suddenly the children, looking down, saw the garden,

with its crowd of women and children all running in the same direction, getting smaller and smaller. In no time, they were almost lost to view in the rain. Then a thick,

black cloud enfolded the travellers. They found themselves in complete darkness. An instant later, a vivid flash of lightning streaked past, seeming to miss them by inches, followed immediately by a deafening clap of thunder.

"That singed my whiskers!" announced the carpet, jovially, as the thunder died away. "Lumme, guv'nor, you ain't 'alf chosen a nice day for an outing! I'd sooner take a beating any day!"

All at once they were out of the cloud, with a bright blue sky above them, and a glorious sun pouring down, making their wet clothes steam with its heat. It was a marvellous feeling. Philip and Mary sat up on the carpet and basked in the warmth. It was like the very best kind of sun bathing. Below and on every side were great clouds, black and grey and white, and ever and again between them were rifts through which they could catch glimpses of the countryside wheeling slowly beneath them, while the carpet, so it seemed, hung suspended in the clear sky, its shadow reflected on the moving clouds.

Presently the clouds disappeared, and they saw that they were sailing along over green fields and woods, roads, railways and houses. Almost at once the houses began to multiply beneath them, the fields disappeared, and there, right ahead, was the golden cross of St. Paul's Cathedral, glistening in the sunlight. The carpet was now coming down at a steep angle, and Philip and Mary held on tight for fear they should slip off.

"You needn't pinch my pile," grumbled the carpet. "I won't let you go." It was heading now for a tall office building standing near St. Paul's, just on the edge of the bare space which the Germans left when they tried to burn London down.

"Third floor!" said Sir Sigismund sharply, as the building loomed in front of them like a cliff.

"O.K.!" muttered the carpet. One of the windows on the third floor was open. Rolling up its sides to make itself narrower, it flew straight for the window. The children ducked frantically and shut their eyes as they scraped narrowly between the sill and the sash. Almost immediately they felt that they were flying no longer. There was a hard floor beneath them and the carpet was stretched out flat and lifeless. They opened their eyes and stood up. Looking round, they found themselves in a large, bare room. There were two desks in it, covered with great leatherbound ledgers, and a smaller table with a typewriter. Behind each desk sat a spectacled clerk, one elderly and one quite youthful, while behind the table was a gaily dressed young woman, her fingers on the keys of the typewriter. One and all sat up and stared with all their might at the new arrivals, but none of them uttered a word. Quite obviously they literally could not believe their eyes, and each of them thought that what he saw must be invisible to the others. The elder clerk opened his mouth to speak, changed his mind, coughed, ran his finger between his collar and his neck, and then got up and opened the window a little wider (which was just what the children wanted). The younger one shook his head, blinked, and pulling a small bottle and a glass out of his desk, poured himself out a drink with a shaking hand. As for the typist, she put her hand to her head for a moment and then produced a bottle of aspirin from her bag. When she had swallowed one she set to work to type at furious speed, without once glancing again at the carpet with its three passengers right under her nose.

"Wait here," said Sir Sigismund quietly to the two children, as he scrambled to his feet. "I'm going to give MacSwindle the shock of his wicked life."

From his pocket he produced the cheque which Philip had returned to him, and flourishing this in his hand he walked across the room to a door marked "PRIVATE". He opened it without knocking and went straight through. Looking after him, Philip and Mary could see into a small room, with a large desk in it, placed endways to the door. On one side of the desk was seated a lean, pale man with very small pig-like eyes and a mouth that might have been drawn with a ruler, so hard and straight and thin was it. On the other side was their father, and the desk between them was covered with papers. Both men looked up in astonishment as Sir Sigismund strode in. Then the door closed behind him, and the children were left standing on the carpet, surrounded by the clerks, who were still busy pretending they were not there.

They had not long to wait. In two or three minutes Sir Sigismund came out again, rubbing his hands in glee.

"That's that!" he said. "And one of the best bits of business I've ever done in my life! Your father's got nothing to worry about now, and I've left MacSwindle with a nasty headache. You'd better be off now before your father sees you. I must get back to my office."

"Shall I drop you there, sir?" said the carpet, suddenly coming to life.

"No thanks," said Sir Sigismund, stepping nimbly off it as it rose from the floor. "I'll take a taxi. It'll look better. Take these children back to their grandmother's, will you?"

"O.K.," said the carpet, and began to glide slowly towards the window.

"Oh please, just a minute!" Mary called out.

"What is it?" asked Sir Sigismund, catching the carpet by its edge before it could fly away.

"May I have a wish, please?"

"M'm, I'm not sure you're entitled to one by the regulations. I thought you'd had enough of wishes, anyway. What do you want?"

"It's quite an easy wish, Sir Sigismund," said Mary. "It's just, if it was allowed, I should like to wish for a bicycle."

"A bicycle? Good gracious me, if this invention of your father's is half what I think it is, he'll be able to give you all the bicycles you want, and motor-cars, too. You don't want a wish for that."

"But it's not for me," Mary explained. "It's for Mr. Chaffers. If it hadn't been for him, we'd never have got the bottle back, and I know he does miss his bicycle dreadfully. May I wish for that, please?"

Sir Sigismund nodded and smiled, "I'll see to it," he said.

He let go of the carpet and an instant later they found themselves soaring up above the roof-tops of the City.

The journey home was quick and uneventful. Far too soon for the children's enjoyment they were flying over the garden at Bolster Place, now once more shining in the sunlight after the storm. As they came down towards the front door, Philip thought of something.

"I say," he said to the carpet, "would you mind doing something for us?"

"As if I 'adn't done nothing already," grumbled the carpet. "What's the great idea, cock?"

"Do you think you could possibly make yourself a bit shorter, so as to fit the hall?" Philip asked. "About six inches would do, I should think. I know it's been worrying Granny terribly."

"Suits me," said the carpet. "I 'ate being rumpled up, anyway. It's un'ealthy. And there's a worn patch in my middle I wouldn't mind getting rid of at all. 'Ere goes!"

As it swooped through the door the children felt the carpet beneath them shrug itself just below where they were sitting. Then, with a sigh of relief, it settled down in its old place in the hall and became an ordinary Turkey carpet once more. But this time it fitted the space left for it as perfectly as though it had been made for that very purpose.

As Philip and Mary stood up, Mrs. Thwaites came into the hall from the drawing-room.

"So you've got here, children!" she said. "Did you manage to find somewhere to keep dry during that awful storm? You're just in time for tea. It's been a bit delayed, Susan had an accident with the tray. Most unlike her, but I suppose the thunder scared her. Oh!" she exclaimed suddenly, as she noticed the carpet. "Mr. Chaffers, however did you manage it? Mr. Chaffers! Where are you, Mr. Chaffers!"

Mr. Chaffers came down the stairs, looking rather puzzled. He had a hammer in his hand and several two inch wire nails in his mouth.

"Mr. Chaffers, you really are a magician," Mrs. Thwaites said to him. "I noticed when I came in you had taken the carpet up to see what could be done with it, and here it is again already, fitting exactly. How did you do it so quickly?"

Mr. Chaffers took the nails out of his mouth, scratched his head and then decided to say "Ah!" in a most mysterious voice. On the whole, it was probably the wisest thing he could say in all the circumstances. But he said "Ah!" again, much louder and with enormous satisfaction, when two or three days later a superb new three-speed bicycle was delivered at his house, with a label tied to it, saying, "With the compliments of Sir Sigismund Kaufman-Fortescue, D.D., and of Master and Miss Jelf."

Mr. Jelf was extremely talkative that evening.

"Do you know, dear," he said to his wife, after the children had gone to bed, "when Sir Sigismund walked into MacSwindle's office, I felt as though I was in a dream! So much so, that I had a positive hallucination."

"A what, George?"

"A—how shall I describe it?—a kind of vision. I could see Sir Sigismund, of course, but behind him I seemed to see, through a sort of mist, the dear ones he had come to save from poverty."

"George, darling! Do you really mean you had a vision of me?"

"Er—no," Mr. Jelf confessed. "Not actually of you, dear. I don't know why it should be, but you weren't part of it. But I did see the children quite clearly, looking at me as I sat there."

"Well," said Mrs. Jelf in a rather disappointed tone, 'visions or no visions, I must finish checking their clothes or packing to-morrow. I'm afraid it has been rather a dull holiday for them, poor things!"

"Yes," Mr. Jelf agreed. "Very dull indeed!"

Made in the USA
Coppell, TX
22 December 2020

46939803R00094